FALCONER AND THE FACE OF GOD

An unputdownable medieval mystery with a twist

IAN MORSON

William Falconer Medieval Mysteries Book 3

JOFFE
Ostara
CLASSICS

Revised edition 2023
Joffe Books, London
www.joffebooks.com

First published in Great Britain in 1996

This paperback edition was first published
in Great Britain in 2023

This book is a work of fiction. Names, characters, businesses, organizations, places and events are either the product of the author's imagination or are used fictitiously. Any resemblance to actual persons, living or dead, events or locales is entirely coincidental.
The spelling used is British English except where fidelity to the author's rendering of accent or dialect supersedes this.

Cover art by Nick Castle

ISBN: 978-1-83526-250-4

ACKNOWLEDGEMENT

The verses at the beginning of each chapter are taken from a modern English adaptation of the Chester Mystery Plays by Maurice Hussey, published by William Heinemann in 1957.

PROLOGUE

Abraham and Isaac strode up to the hill that stood before them. The old man's words to his son belied what was in his heart — the sacrifice of the youth.

'Now, Isaac my son, wend we our way
To yonder mountain, if that we may.'

They stood at the foot of the flat green bank, which appeared to be no more than a crudely daubed shape on a cloth that flapped idly in the threatening wind. There was a storm in the air, and Isaac sensed something wrong.

'There, 'tis on the ground at last
But father why are you downcast?
Is there something that you dread?
Father, as it is your will,
Where is the beast that we shall kill?'

Abraham seemed to stumble over his next words and repeated what he had said. His son feigned not to notice, but, glancing apprehensively at the gathering clouds over their heads, voiced his fear.

'Father, it makes me sore afraid
To see you wield a naked blade.
I fear your hand may not be stayed,
And you may kill your faithful child.'

Powerless to intervene, the watching throng shivered at the scene that was being played out before their eyes. They had witnessed it many times before, but the outcome always seemed in doubt each time. Would old Abraham truly slay his son? He spoke out to the heavens, which sent a chill wind to whip through his long, white locks.

'Isaac, Isaac, I must thee kill!'

Isaac was curiously resigned.

'Alas! Father, is that your will,
Your own child's blood to spill?'
'Oh, my dear son,' cried Abraham, 'I'm sorry
To lay this burden on thee.
'Tis God's commandment on me,
And his works are ever right.'

Spots of rain began to speckle the wooden boards of the cart on which Gyles de Multon stood. He decided he had better hurry through Isaac's words before the rain started in earnest and drowned them all — actors and audience alike. He prodded a surreptitious thumb at the sky — a message intended for John Peper only to see — and plunged on.

'Seeing that I must needs be dead,
Of one thing I will you pray
When you do the deed today,
Use as few strokes as well you may,
When you strike off my head.'

John Peper, in the role of Abraham, led Gyles over to the chest that normally held small items they used on stage, now serving as the sacrificial altar. He glanced nervously over to the side of the staging where the Archangel lay in waiting. The wind whipped the side-cloth across the entrance and he could see nothing. He pressed on.

'To do this deed I am most sorry
And Lord to thee I cry,
On his soul please have mercy,
For it has always been true.'

Gyles lay back, the spots of rain now hitting his face.

'O father, father, why do you tarry so?
Smite off my head and let me go.
I pray you rid me of my woe,
And now I take my leave of you.'

John Peper raised the heavy sword over his head, above the exposed neck of Gyles de Multon. God's 'sacrifice' gave him an exaggerated wink, not visible to the crowd below the tableau. Peper stifled a guffaw at his comrade's unseemly act and brought the blunt but lethal weapon down in a sweeping arc, confident that it would be stopped before it did any harm. But the expected intervention did not occur, and John Peper blanched as the blade cut deep into the flesh of his friend. He wrenched the weapon away to reveal a gaping wound in the soft white skin at Gyles's neck, which soon pulsed scarlet with his life's blood. A stifled gasp escaped Peper's lips, and he staggered back, dropping the bloody sword with a clatter at his feet.

The cheers from the crowd were strangled when a fountain of blood spouted from Isaac's neck. Everyone in the audience had seen the tableau before and knew the story line by line. This was not supposed to happen. Those at the front of the press pushed backwards in horror as gouts of blood splashed over their clothes. They had come in holiday mood, dressed in their finest gowns, which were now being ruined. On the wagon, which was decked out as a hillside in the Holy Land, Gyles de Multon clutched at the gaping wound in his neck, rolled off the crudely built altar and staggered the few steps to the edge of the platform. His lips moved but no sound came from them as, uncomprehending, he fell at the feet of the retreating mob. His eyes turned up to heaven in astonishment before they clouded over for ever. At that very moment a flash of lightning rent the clouds and the skies opened, the rain washing the rivers of blood from the stage.

CHAPTER ONE

GOD: I am Alpha and Omega,
Foremost and noblest.
Being my will it should be so,
It is, it was, and shall be thus.

The Fall of Lucifer

The priory church of St Frideswide was full of townsfolk. Sweat ran off expectant faces, well-wrapped bodies were pressed close against each other. Still, it was fortunate that brewer was crammed shoulder to shoulder with skinner's wife, and fuller's mistress with bootmaker, for it was the depths of winter and, empty, the church would have been freezing. Today, the icy cold outside was driven back by the heat of body pressed on body as everyone jostled for a better view. Even the aisle was a mêlée of merchants and their wives, elbowing one another aside in eager anticipation.

There was a movement near the high altar, an intonation of some Latin verse, and the crowd surged forward, impelled by those at the back. They could see little, if anything at all, and were anxious not to miss the miracle. This was an event they had waited for all year. Hadn't the King himself worshipped at the shrine of the saint only two years ago? True, the barons led by de Montfort had imprisoned the King soon after. But not for long — only last year the King had been restored to his people and de Montfort had been cut into little pieces on the battlefield. The saint had truly looked after Henry, who was now in his fiftieth year on the throne. And now their only chance at snatching a little of his luck was jeopardized by the press of others less fastidious than themselves. Some had simply forced their way to the front in a scrimmage of elbows. Those who had been pushed away grumbled about their misfortune and wondered how the winners in the scramble could behave so grossly in the house of God.

There was a gasp from those at the front as the casket containing the mortal remains of St Frideswide was transferred from her shrine to the high altar.

'What happened? Did you see?'

Those at the rear anxiously questioned those in front of them, asking if a miracle had occurred. These in their turn asked those ahead of them. The murmur of voices carried the query to the front of the close-packed crowd, and a message was returned in hushed tones by the same route. Some right at the back were still uncertain.

'Was there a miracle?'

'I think he said there was a vision of the saint.'

'No, no. Someone over there said the water in the chalice truly had been turned into wine.'

'They say there's a blind man who can now see.'

This last hissed comment caused a gabble of excitement around the speaker, even though this miracle was attributed to St Frideswide at least twice a year, on her feast day in October, and as now at Christmastide. The saint's own story told of the prince who sought to overcome her vow of virginity and was struck blind in punishment. His sight was restored by the saint when he renounced his evil plan. Now the blind made pilgrimages to her church, in the hope of being able to see once again. And it did happen — everyone knew of a blind man whose sight had been restored. Though no one could ever name him or point such a one out if asked.

Right at the back of the press of the good townsfolk of Oxford stood Edward Petysance, priest of St Aldate's Church. He skulked sourly behind the last pillar in the powerful row that tied the flying arches of the roof to humble earth. Although the massive door of the south-west entrance was closed against the weather, an icy draught whistled through the gaps in the door's imperfect fit. It cut through Petysance's thick woollen robe like a shaft of cold steel and, move as he might, he could not avoid the edge of its searching blade. He shivered, and angrily pushed against the bodies around him, but to no avail. The sharp elbow of a scrawny harridan was thrust into his soft belly, and she gave him a fleeting glance of toothless ire before she returned to peering over the heads in front of her.

Petysance gave up, and lifting the heavy latch slipped out through the door, leaving it open as a lesson in tolerance to the ugly woman whose elbow had all but pierced his gut. The frozen ridges of mud crackled under his feet as he made his way back across the courtyard, and into Fish Street and his spartan quarters in the shadow of St Aldate's Church. The weakened sun, which had hardly taken the chill off the day in its lugubrious crawl across the sky, was already dipping below the line of the new city walls. With Christmas fast approaching, other citizens of Oxford were preparing themselves for the celebrations that would mark a turn in the winter's icy grip. But Petysance was in no mood for jollification.

He was consumed with jealousy for the Prior of St Frideswide, whose life was made so comfortable because of his ownership of a set of bones. Kings, clerics and commoners flocked to the Prior's church to worship in the presence of the saint's holy relics, while at St Aldate's he struggled, with increasing difficulty, to maintain the fabric of God's building entrusted to his care. And did the Prior have such problems? Indeed no — with bursting coffers, he squandered coin on bigger buildings. It was but ten years since the Prior had crowned his edifice with a new bell-lantern and spire. A taunting pinnacle that Petysance could not avoid seeing every time he looked through the east window of his church.

He slammed the door on the unfair world outside his chilly rooms and leaned back against it, groaning in frustration. If only he possessed a similar attraction for the pilgrim — a relic of some sort was all he required. A vial of Christ's blood, a single saintly limb, a finger-bone even, and he would be satisfied. But he had nothing.

* * *

John Peper's hand shook as he poured the water, stained red with paint, into the glass vial on the bench. The liquid splashed across the rough wooden surface, and the pitcher slipped from his fingers, shattering on the floor of the wagon. The counterfeit blood dribbled through the gaps in the planking, but all John could see was the face of his friend Gyles staring up at him in incomprehension. He gasped and held his trembling palms out in front of him. They were red with Gyles's blood. A woman's plain but friendly face was thrust through the gap in the curtain that enclosed the wagon's interior. Seeing the state that John was in, and guessing the cause, she stepped through the heavy arras. Clasping his hands in her own chapped but gentle palms, she tried to console him as she had frequently done over the last few weeks.

'Agnes, I saw his face again. Why does he hate me so?'

The peasant woman's voice was surprisingly soft.

'Gyles doesn't hate you. It was not your fault.'

'Then why does he haunt me so?'

Peper's query came out as a high-pitched squeal, like a hare caught in a snare. Agnes wiped away the tears and snot that ran down his contorted face. Her voice hardened in anger as she comforted him.

'It's not you Gyles should be haunting, it's Stefano. It was his fault, after all. He insisted you use a real blade — we'd always used a wooden one before. And he should have stopped the blade — he was the Angel Gabriel for that performance, wasn't he? If anyone should be blamed for Gyles's death, it's Stefano.'

A harsh and vengeful look crept over her homely features and she squeezed John's arm tight. For a moment it frightened him, then the look was gone. Snivelling, John Peper turned back to the bench at which he had been working and started mopping up the spilt liquid with an old rag that at one time had been the Archangel's robe. Agnes squatted down and began to pick up the shattered pieces of the pitcher from the floor.

'He shouldn't have made you do this, anyway — filling bottles with coloured water so he can sell them as holy blood to the fools who come to see us. Can't he see you're still upset?'

She looked up at Peper's broad back, which shuddered as another convulsion of misery enveloped him, and mumbled to herself, 'And we all know where he was instead of being set to come on stage.'

* * *

Stefano de Askeles was at that very moment planning where he should take his troupe of jongleurs next. The purses of those who frequented the inns of Abingdon had proved tighter than he had hoped. Perhaps the tale of their little bit of bad luck in Winchester had followed them here already. When they had first arrived, Simon Godrich's lascivious songs had gone down well in the taverns. And Margaret's tumbling had most of the men agog. Dressed in men's breeches, her lithe figure as it sprung, rolled and contorted left little to her audience's imagination. Which was just as well, as few of the stupid labourers who filled the hat with coins had any imagination to exercise. Of all the women saltatores de Askeles had seen in his life, Margaret Peper was the most supple and graceful. She was wasted on her husband, and de Askeles only employed him to keep Margaret in his troupe of players.

And her body was not only pliant on stage or in the taverns. De Askeles grinned as he recalled the contortions she had performed solely for him the previous evening, while he had kept her husband busy mixing the 'holy blood'.

All their good fortune, however, seemed to have trickled away in the last few days, and it was clearly time to move on. Calculating that Christmastide would soon be upon them, he decided the time was right to make their way to Oxford. The monks or the merchant guilds there would be mounting the annual mystery plays and could easily be persuaded to use his troupe's professional skills. And the carefree nature of the students always guaranteed loose purse-strings, even amongst such a normally impecunious mob. He would arrange for a message to be sent to the Prior of St Frideswide and the leaders of the guilds to alert them to his arrival. There was nothing like a little anticipation to raise people's level of eagerness for entertainment. Yes, Oxford at Christmas it would be — why, the King might even be there. Then the money would really begin to flow.

* * *

There was an unusual state of panic in the Chancellor's residence at Oxford. The present incumbent of the office, Henry de Cicestre, was a fastidious man and preparations for the festival would normally have been well advanced, but a few days earlier de Cicestre had received a message that his elderly mother had been taken ill. In a flurry of activity, the Chancellor had got himself ready and departed for her home in Southampton. Halegod, the chief steward of de Cicestre's household and of many chancellors' before him, had therefore looked forward to a lazy Christmastide. No fussy master to run around after, no meals to supervise except his own. He had thought he might even arrange for his own feast to be charged up to the Chancellor's tally. He had mouth-watering dreams of roast curlew or woodcock with oysters, to be followed by his favourite dish of seethed figs and ale.

Then de Cantilupe had literally turned up on the doorstep. When Halegod unsuspectingly opened the door, the former Chancellor had swept in and occupied the residence as though two years and the death of Baron Simon had not happened. Halegod was back to being ordered about, and his vision of a sybaritic Christmas dissipated. Grumbling, he set about lighting the fire as Thomas de Cantilupe settled in what had been his favourite chair before leaving Oxford. In the intervening two years he had effectively sided with Simon de Montfort in his struggle with Henry III, and for a short time had been rewarded with the Chancellorship of England. Unfortunately, Baron Simon's ascendancy had been brief, and within a year Thomas had found himself on the wrong side. Luckily, he had always retained a good relationship with Prince Edward, Henry's son, and had not been dispossessed as many of the rebel barons had been. Now he had heard that the King was to spend his Christmas in Oxford, and planned to ingratiate himself back into the favour of the victor of the Barons' Wars.

With the departure of the present Chancellor from the scene, it seemed perfectly reasonable to de Cantilupe to occupy his residence. After all, it had been his own until a few years ago. And looking round, he saw that the parsimonious de Cicestre had not exactly put his hand into his purse to furnish the house. The wall hangings were those that de Cantilupe had purchased — a little shabbier now, but still serviceable. Even the furniture was the same, with the familiar stains and scratches that he had made himself. He sighed and wrapped his fur robe around his cold limbs as Halegod grovelled at his feet, blowing life into the feeble flickerings in the hearth. It all seemed like a step backwards, but then sometimes you had to retreat to go forwards again. He knew this was a critical time for him.

* * *

In one of the more imposing stone houses in the centre of Oxford, an old man sat poring over an ancient text. His thin, cadaverous frame was hunched in the chair, and his shallow but rapid breath froze in the chill of the unheated room. Despite the cold, though, he felt feverish and sweat ran down his domed forehead from the line of straggly hair that clung to his balding pate. More sweat from his palms stained the already much thumbed volume. That morning he had woken up to recall fragments of a dream in which he had tried to run away from a cloud of bees that had inexplicably entered his house. In the dream his legs were like the trunks of a tree — rooted to the spot — and he could not escape the buzzing swarm. As they descended on him and began to sting, he woke with a start to realize the day was already well advanced, and the sun was streaming through the window arch of his bedchamber. His bedclothes were twisted around his limbs and damp with sweat.

He had risen, dressing hurriedly, and scurried to the stack of texts he kept in the main room on the ground floor of his house. Little sunlight penetrated here in the winter owing to both the low sun and the close press of houses, and it did not help that the shutters were closed tight. He struggled across the darkened room and at first in his haste he could not find what he wanted. Then he saw part of the title written in his own hand on the vellum cover jutting out from the bottom of a pile of books: . . . *Abecedarii Danielis Prophete*.

In his haste he tipped the stack of texts on to the floor before he retrieved the one he wanted from the heap scattered on the rushes — the Book of Dreams according to the ABC of Daniel the Prophet. Thumbing through the pages he had confirmed what he feared. Both the swarm of bees and being unable to run were portents of evil in themselves. To have them both together was a cause for grave concern, and on the very day he had decided to try out the next stage of his experiment to create the quintessence. Perhaps his experiment would blow up in his face, perhaps the warning was about something else he could not foresee. The spectre of death loomed large in his mind, but whether his own, or a death caused by him, was not clear. Still, he always trusted the warnings from his dream world, and decided he would consult Hermes before he began. He hurried down to the cellar to set up the altar.

* * *

The wagon ground its ponderous way along the icy road between Abingdon and Oxford. The breath of the two horses that pulled it steamed out of their nostrils and mingled with the whitish trails of mist that obscured any view the occupants of the wagon might have had of the passing countryside. They were locked in a frozen landscape, silently huddled down against the bleak weather. John Peper sat up front, guiding the horses' steady plod through the crackling mud. Next to him sat the two women — Margaret, and Agnes Cheke, feeling awkward at the strained atmosphere between husband and wife. Margaret's raven hair was tucked under the woollen scarf that was wound tightly round her head and neck. Her slender figure was muffled in layers of clothing topped by the crimson, fur-lined cloak that Stefano sometimes wore as God in the pageants.

Margaret Peper was deep in thought, keeping boredom and the cold, depressing weather at bay by reviewing her life. She could not remember a time when she had not been dependent on someone, usually a man, for sustenance. She had never known her mother, who it was said had died giving birth to her. And her father had sold her to an acrobat when she was barely seven years old. The acrobat had taught her his skills and then she had toured the country in his company. He had convinced her that she should be grateful to him for the very bread she ate, and she didn't question it in later years when she did all the work and he simply collected their earnings from the crowds she drew. By then he had grown stiff-jointed, his once muscled limbs becoming knobbly at the knee and elbow. But his manner was such that she did not challenge his taking the lion's share of the money. After all, he kept reminding her, he had taught her and fed her when she was of no immediate value to him. She paid for that training by succumbing to his advances when she was barely old enough to understand what he was doing to her, as well as by entertaining the crowds with acrobatic feats. Then one morning she had woken to the sound of the birds singing in the trees — as usual they were sleeping under the stars — and he had not responded to her voice. She tried to shake him awake, but he was stiff and cold. The old acrobat had died in the night. She might have then found her independence, but as fate would have it she met up with John Peper two days later. He had seen her perform and realized she was exceptional at her art as well as being beautiful. But she was struggling to work on her own, as she had no one to collect money from the crowd as she carried out her saltatorial contortions. When she stopped to collect, the crowd drifted away. Quickly John had taken off his hat and made the collection for her. They decided to work together though John had no particular skills, and they had eventually married almost for convenience's sake. They had still struggled to make enough money to live until she had been spotted by de Askeles. Now, having joined de Askeles's troupe, Margaret was dependent on another man for her continued survival. And the conflict between pleasing her husband and satisfying de Askeles was proving troublesome. If only she was rid of one of them. She was brought back to the real world by Agnes's head nodding on to her shoulder, and she sighed.

Robert Kemp, the juggler, and Simon Godrich, goliard, trudged gloomily beside the horses, trying to benefit from the heat that radiated from their flanks. Their idle thoughts were turned to Gyles, a good and long-time friend, now dead thanks to de Askeles's carelessness: Both in their own ways contemplated what they might do. The simpleton, Will Plome, hung from the side of the wagon, mirroring the posture of the monkey that sat huddled in the cage that swayed between the wagon wheels. His thoughts were no more focused than those of the huddled beasts in the fields they passed.

Inside the wagon was a magical world of stars and moons, shiny swords and parti-coloured caps with bells, piled on top of rolled-up sheets that hinted at exotic forests and bubbling clouds. Viols bumped against tabors and, suspended from the canvas walls, empty-eyed masks rocked from side to side. They resembled some hellish assembly of brainless beasts mournfully shaking their heads at human pleading. Snug and warm in the centre of this cornucopia was tucked Stefano de Askeles, befuddled with wine, ensconced on the throne he used in his role as God. He was snoring and the sound carried out to the ears of John Peper on his perch behind the horses' rumps. Each rasping snore grated in John's head, and he ground his teeth in anguish.

His gaze was fixed on the backs of the scrawny nags that pulled the overloaded wagon, but he didn't really see them. In his mind's eye he had Abraham's sword in his hand, the blade razor sharp and sparkling in the sun. He swung it high above Isaac, but instead of his friend Gyles de Multon the sacrifice was Stefano de Askeles. The master of the troupe tried to move, but John had bound him with real knots, rather than the fake ones he had always used on Gyles. Stefano's eyes widened in panic and he tried to plead with John, but no sound escaped his trembling lips. John tightened his grasp on the horses' reins, and in his imagination swung the sword down in a deadly arc on to de Askeles's exposed neck. His head was abruptly severed, and rolled across the stage as his life's blood spurted from the twitching body.

CHAPTER TWO

ANGELS: We thank thee, Lord in sovereignty
That us hath made so clean and clear,
Ever in this bliss to abide with Thee.
Grant us thy grace to live ever here.

The Fall of Lucifer

'Consider this statement — whatever runs has legs. Agreed?'

The students, whose ages ranged from a spotty fifteen to an awkward eighteen, all nodded in agreement. Their clothes were as various as their ages. Some were dressed in long fashionable robes of many colours, made from silks and other rich materials. Some were clad in simple, short tunics of drab brown fustian. It would be foolish to say that all were equals in the eyes of the university — some were destined for high office, and some would struggle to obtain a country living. But at the moment all that mattered was the quickness of their brains, and in that, a farmer's son could outstrip the offspring of the King's Chancellor.

This was the last day of their first term at the university, and they all already thought themselves masters of logic. The regent master nodded his grizzled head of grey hair in response to their agreement, and rubbed his raw, mitten-clad hands together to drive away the cold. He paced up and down the aisle in the midst of the eager faces.

'Then consider this statement — the River Thames runs. Therefore . . .'

The final part of his fallacious syllogism was drowned out by twenty piping voices.

'The River Thames has legs.'

The joke was old but the young men still fell about laughing at the proposition. This was the last *dies legibilis*, formal day of lectures, before Christmastide and there was an expectant mood of enjoyment and of future pleasures. The regent master ruefully shook his head, and grinned, exhaling a misty cloud of breath into the chilly schoolroom. He calmed the noisy rabble with a wave of his hands and concluded the lecture.

'Go away now and read Aristotle's *Posterior Analytics*. You will see that all syllogisms require a process of experience by the senses, *intellectus*, as well as *scientia*, knowledge. Only by personal experience can you resolve the puzzle of a syllogism. Therefore the whole process is classed as deduction.'

Deduction. The entire class, though new to Oxford, was aware this was the regent master's obsession. They had already heard from older students that he frequently tested his deductive abilities in the most practical of syllogistic puzzles. It was said that no murder in Oxford had remained unresolved since he came to the town. This fact filled them with awe for the big, ungainly-looking man of unconventional habits, and they sat silently under his piercing blue gaze until one nervous youth broke the spell.

'Master Falconer, may we leave now?'

As though jerked back to reality from a dream world, William Falconer grunted his dismissal, and waved the students away with his bony hands.

'Go and enjoy your Christmas wherever you are bound. But don't forget to read your texts also.'

As he gathered his own books from the raised desk he rarely sat at, preferring to be on a level with his students, the youths scrambled for the door. Some were bound for their family homes for Christmas, but most would stay in Oxford. Either their homes were too far to travel to and from in the short break, or they were simply too poor to make the journey. Those staying behind had already been forewarned that Christmas in Oxford was a lively time, when songs were sung and stories told. The students' halls could be unruly, boisterous places when election of a Lord of Misrule turned the accepted order of the world upside down for a day. The master in charge of the hall might even allow in strolling players to perform their mummery, or get the students to enact scenes themselves. And there was always plenty to drink. Some of the youths leaving Falconer's lecture were already testing their singing voices, mingling lovers' songs with carols.

'Oh, my heart is true, for Mary she said so;' sang one pimply lad, who seemed barely capable of arousing anything other than mother love in a woman. Two others were rendering a harmonious anthem of rejoicing as they disappeared down the muddy alley.

'Make we merry in hall and bower,
This time was born our Saviour.'

For Falconer the break presented an opportunity to work some more on the scientific texts he fancied incorporating into one document. He had even thought of a title — *Summa Philosophiae* — though he was concerned it might be a little pretentious. To date he had written treatises on the nature of light, celestial spheres, and stones and minerals, in which he had incorporated much of the fragmentary material smuggled out of France from his close friend Friar Roger Bacon. He had not seen the man for more than ten years, since the Franciscan general, John of Fidenza, had virtually imprisoned the friar in 1257. His outspoken views on the nature of the world had not endeared him to his order. Some condemned him as a magician. To Falconer he was a towering thinker, and he was afraid his ideas might be lost to the world. This fear had spurred him on to writing his own *Summa*, borrowing freely from the incarcerated friar.

He sighed and closed the door on the tiny lecture room he rented in the ramshackle two-storey building in Schools Street. He was beginning to wonder why he was still teaching at Oxford. He was much older than most of the other regent masters, who lectured, as each must after being incepted as a master, only for a few years before finding a lucrative benefice somewhere, or service in the King's household as a clerk. He had wasted years pursuing other, ephemeral goals before he came to formal learning late in life. Had those years been truly wasted, though? Did he not know more about the world than any of his colleagues closeted in this cosy world of study? He had asked himself those questions many times and come up with many answers — none entirely satisfactory. But here he was approaching his fifth decade, and still barely surviving on the meagre benefice the Abbot of Oseney supplied, plus the few pennies per student per year the lectures provided. Was it all worth it?

Crossing the High Street diagonally in front of the newly completed St Mary's Church, he was about to turn down Grope Lane when he heard his name called. Surreptitiously he drew his eye-lenses from the purse at his hip, and held the V-shaped device to his forehead. Looking through the glass lenses fixed at the ends of the two arms, he brought the blurred street around him into focus. His eyes had deteriorated some years ago through poring over crabbed texts in the light of a flickering candle. More recently he had been overjoyed to have his vision restored by the artifice of Samson the Jew, who had created this eye-lens device.

The figure he saw swimming into focus was that of one of the students from his hall, Aristotle's: Hugh Pett, soon to complete his course of study and become a master himself. Unusually for Hugh, who was normally well coiffured and conscious of his own gravitas, his red hair was dishevelled and his sumptuous green robe hitched up in his fist so that he could run at full pelt down the muddy street.

'Master, wait.'

Falconer indicated that he had seen the young man, and dropped the lenses back into his purse. Pett slid to a halt in front of him, gasping for breath. The regent master smiled gently and took his arm.

'Now what is the occasion of all this haste? Could it not have waited until I returned?'

'A message,' gasped Hugh.

'A message that could not wait a few more hours?'

'It's delivered by a friar. A Franciscan friar from Paris. He says the message is from Friar Bacon.'

* * *

It was because John Peper was bound up in his own world of retribution that the robbers came so close to taking the jongleurs' lives and hard-earned money. As the wagon creaked its way through the gloom of Bagley Wood, John was too engrossed to see the tell-tale marks of footprints etched in the frosty grass of the clearing ahead. Normally he would have whipped up the horses at such an obvious trap, but pleasurable thoughts of Stefano's head rolling in the filth of a muddy street in Oxford distracted him. The heavy wagon even slowed further as the horses strained to haul it through a particularly muddy patch only partly frozen by the coldness of the day. Both Robert and Simon had had enough of walking. They sat wearily on the tailgate of the wagon, dangling their tired legs out of the back, and suffering the drunken declamations of de Askeles from inside.

Suddenly, a burly shape dressed in tattered clothes dropped out of a tree and landed squarely in the lap of a startled Agnes. As she squealed and fell back against an equally surprised Margaret Peper, the robber swung his club at John. Fortunately, John managed to raise his left arm to protect his head, and the brutal blow slid off the fleshy part of his upper arm, tearing the cloth, but only grazing his temple. None the less, he was stunned and the horses came to a standstill as the reins were jerked and let slack. Out of the forest undergrowth appeared several more ill-dressed brigands, all wielding hefty clubs and rusty swords. One of their company, an ugly hunchback with red-rimmed goggling eyes, wrestled with the horses' traces, holding the beasts steady as his comrades-in-arms began to clamber on the wagon. Taken by surprise, the troupe of jongleurs were in disarray.

Margaret lay curled up under the driver's seat as two other robbers clad in rags heaved themselves on to the footboard. Agnes received a ferocious blow in the face. She fell back into the wagon's interior, clutching her bloody nose, all resistance knocked out of her. At the rear of the wagon matters were equally desperate. Simon and Robert had both been thrown backwards from their perch, and Godrich sat up groggily to find Robert Kemp lying ashen-faced and out cold, blood pumping from a gash on his temple. The weather-beaten, scarred features of one of their assailants peered greedily over the rear board, his calloused fingers scrabbling to lift him into the wagon. It promised rich pickings with its store of sumptuous apparel and massive chests tightly bound with leather straps. He smiled coldly and toothlessly at the petrified Godrich, then shoved his weapon between his lips to free his hands. The musician scrabbled for something to defend himself with, his hands finding nothing better than a broken viol smashed as he had fallen on it. Against the vicious implement the robber clenched between his lips, it would be no defence at all.

Then their luck turned. Will Plome was escaping over the side of the wagon and clutched at the nearest thing to hand to help him. It was the cage that housed their monkey. His grasping fingers tore open the door of the cage, and the terrified animal sprang from it, scaling the ropes that had been Will's makeshift hammock. So it was that as one of the brigands went to clamber across the pitched battle on the driver's seat, a hairy demon straight from hell leapt at him, chittering in some outlandish tongue. The demon jumped past him on to the back of the first robber and began tearing at his face. Then another even more fearsome sight loomed up.

Having drunk himself into a stupor, Stefano de Askeles had fixed a mask on his face and begun declaiming lines from a play he imagined he would perform before the King. When the wagon jerked to a halt, he drunkenly rose to his feet and staggered to the front of the wagon, railing at John Peper's poor driving. The mask he had chosen was a grotesque skull with deep, impenetrable eye sockets.

The outlaw, now confronted by the Angel of Death itself, screamed in panic and turned tail. Meanwhile the first robber had leapt from the wagon, flailing his arms at the demon on his back. Seizing the moment, John regained the traces and urged the horses forward. The surprised hunchback was thrown to the ground, and he was trampled beneath the horses' hooves. His screams of pain were cut off as one front wheel lurched over his body. In the back of the wagon, that death-dealing lurch also wrong-footed the red-faced robber threatening Simon Godrich. His toothless mouth opened in a cavernous expression of surprise and he tumbled head over heels over the backboard. His weapon skittered across the floor to lie at the feet of his erstwhile victim.

Though a running man might have caught up with the lumbering nags and their load, the brigands' advantage was lost and they melted into the forest, leaving one of their crew screaming and kicking at the monkey's continued onslaught, and the crushed body of the hunchback face down in the churned-up mud.

The Angel of Death, in the form of a drunken de Askeles, slumped back into the interior of the wagon, and all John heard was muffled cursing at his ham-fisted driving. He looked sidelong at the two shaking women, who clutched each other in terror, and burst into uproarious laughter as relief flooded through him. Margaret shrieked as something thudded on the canvas of the wagon above their heads, then she joined in the laughter as the hairy face of the monkey peered down at them.

'Tonight you deserve a feast, Ham,' called John, as he eased the wagon down a slope out of the trees, and into the valley of the River Thames.

* * *

The wintry days were extremely short, and the grey overhang of cloud on this day made it seem as though it was already closing, although sext had only just passed, and half of the day was left. But the gloom could not dampen the excitement felt by Regent Master William Falconer. He shook the solemn friar vigorously by the hand, his enormous fist in danger of crushing the little cleric's fingers. Towering over him, he pointed the friar down the narrow street in the direction of South Gate from where he might find the quarters of the Franciscan brotherhood in Oxford. The friar could find temporary accommodation there.

As he watched the slight figure disappear into the darkness, the import of his message echoed round his brain. Roger Bacon was back in favour, with no less a figure than the Pope himself. Clement IV had encouraged the released Franciscan friar to record his knowledge, and Bacon had been working for almost a year already on the work he was calling his *Opus Majus* — his great work.

Falconer closed the door to Aristotle's Hall and wondered just how much freedom his friend now had. It seemed from what the friar said that Bacon was no longer confined to his tiny cell, but still was only free to walk the grounds of the monastery where he had been held for so long. But then he had always lived largely inside his own skull, and Falconer was sure his incarceration had merely fuelled the engine of his thinking. Ironically, William for his part felt himself stifled by the relative freedom he enjoyed. To supplement his earnings, he ran the *domus scholarum* of Aristotle's Hall, and under its roof lived a dozen or so students, some sharing the six rooms that sat snugly under the steeply pitched slate roof atop the two-storey building. Fifty years ago the house and its companions would have been all timber, but a series of disastrous fires had resulted in the richer members of the community building at least the ground floors of their properties in stone. Falconer was not rich, but his landlord the Abbot of Oseney was, and he had the priest to thank for the sturdy construction of Aristotle's. Unlike many of his neighbours,

Falconer did not use the back yard to keep chickens or a pig — neither he nor his students had the inclination. This house and the lecture rooms in Schools Street where, by tradition, the Faculty of Arts taught, was Falconer's world. Was it any larger than Friar Bacon's?

Falconer fingered the letter that the friar had delivered into his hands as he told him of Bacon's change in fortunes. He eagerly read its lines again. Roger Bacon was earnestly seeking Falconer's help on some difficult aspects of that most alluring of modern sciences, alchemy. He waxed lyrical about the 'generation of things from their elements' and the 'rare art of prolonging life'. He made reference to an alchemist who had conducted many experiments of his own, when last Bacon had been in Oxford. Falconer was being asked to seek him out and persuade him to communicate with the exiled friar. He was to give the man a sealed note that had been tucked inside the letter to Falconer. The problem was that Bacon had only given a cryptic clue as to the man's identity.

> *I fear that even now this letter may be intercepted by those inimical to my present status. And to name a fellow scientist outright may equally cause him to fall into disfavour with those whose influence is but temporarily occluded. I trust my description of him makes his name clear to you.*

Bacon ended with an admonition.

> *Remember, dear friend, always hearken to beautiful music, look at beautiful things, have stimulating disputations with sympathetic friends, wear your best clothes and talk to pretty girls.*

The regent master smiled at his friend's wise and typically secular advice. However, he frowned at the puzzle he had been set concerning the Oxford alchemist. Despite Friar Bacon's confidence, he had not the faintest idea to whom the clue in the letter referred. He stowed both letters in his pouch and retired to his solar on the upper floor of Aristotle's Hall.

* * *

The jolt and rumble of the wagon's wheels on hard-packed ground woke the dishevelled de Askeles from his drunken stupor. He groaned as the wagon passed over a deep rut, pitching to one side and sending a spear of pain across his befuddled skull. He lifted the canvas cover between him and the driver's seat and cursed John Peper for his ineptness.

They were passing under the arch of Oxford's South Gate just before the nightly curfew would close the city gates on the dangerous world outside. The flickering light from a brazier in the arch illuminated the group on the front bench of the wagon. John Peper's tensed back drew his head down into his shoulders, and de Askeles could not see his face. He knew his barb had angered Peper, and grinned. The man was so easy to rile, and he enjoyed doing it. As long as Peper needed the work de Askeles gave him, he would endure his vicious words. De Askeles also knew he hurt Peper even more by the attentions he paid his wife. And the man would suffer that too.

Next to Peper sat crazy Agnes Cheke, her bulky, shapeless body made even more so by the bundle of tattered clothes she had pulled around her against the evening chill. She twisted round and pulled an angry face at Stefano, the piggy eyes in her coarsened features seeking to strike him speechless. That look might work on the gullible fools whose fortunes she told, but Stefano had seen it too often.

'Your witch's stare doesn't work on me, pig-face.'

Margaret, sitting on the far side of Agnes, went to put her arm around the woman, but hesitated as Agnes hunched her shoulders and stared stonily away. The young woman returned to the bundle in her lap and cooed as though she had a baby in the warm folds of her skirt. De Askeles leaned roughly over the back of the cowed Agnes and plucked the monkey from where it had snuggled close to Margaret Peper. It squealed in pain as the actor swung it by the tail, its greenish fur bristling at such careless handling. Margaret looked on in shock as de Askeles thrust the wriggling animal at Will Plome, whose anxious face had appeared round the side of the wagon at the first squeal from Ham.

'Cage it!'

The monkey bared its gleaming teeth in fear and leaped into the arms of the youth who cared for it. De Askeles continued to harangue his troupe.

'The animal is too valuable to let loose. It might run away. Tonight, John Peper will make a collar for it and you will keep it on the end of a rope.'

As the wagon rumbled up Fish Street and de Askeles was turning back to the wagon's interior, his gaze lit upon a cadaverous figure that lurked in the darkness of an overhanging doorway. For a moment their eyes met and a sort of recognition flashed between them — the semblancer of Death and one who resembled Death itself. De Askeles shuddered, shook his head, and the figure was gone. His brain thumping, the actor slumped back into the recesses of the wagon, and groped at his feet for the flagon that he had valiantly tried to empty on the journey. He missed the murderous look in Will Plome's eyes as the simpleton stroked the frightened monkey's coat in an attempt to calm it. De Askeles was oblivious of the hatred he engendered in those around him — a fact which was to prove fatal.

CHAPTER THREE

ARCHANGELS: Here to abide God grant us grace
To please this Prince without a peer;
Him now to thank with great solace
A song now let us sing together.

The Fall of Lucifer

Well before darkness fell, the firewood sellers at South Gate began to lock their bundles securely away in the stalls that lined Fish Street. They were soon followed by the fishmongers, whose strong-smelling salty wares were shovelled back into their boxes for the morrow. The narrow shop frontages of the tanners and glove-makers were barred, and the honest citizens retired behind their solid oaken doors. The night watch, a band of robust but aged fellows, performed a circuit of the walls that hemmed in the press of dwellings. At each of the gates the leader of the band selected a massive key from a bunch and locked the burghers safe inside their walls. Some less salubrious citizens were also effectively locked out, for Oxford had already spilled beyond its walls, and the notorious stews outside both North and South Gates were populated with beggars, thieves and easy women.

Soon the wide avenues that cut the walled city into four uneven segments were quiet save for the stirrings of another population: the skittering of the rats and mice that fed on the discarded rubbish of the throng of humanity that flocked the streets by day. But even these denizens of the dark did not have the night-time world to themselves. Long winter evenings guaranteed a plague of boredom amongst the young and lively students who inhabited the numerous halls of Oxford. Moreover, the location of the city at a crossroads of commerce ensured the place also housed a shifting throng of artisans, officials and merchants. A volatile mix of spendthrift youth and wealthy travellers seeking to while away their evenings filled the meanest of back-street taverns in St Martin's with noise and excitement every night.

For Stefano de Askeles and his troupe, this meant but one thing — money, and plenty of it. With their wagon safely stowed in the yard of the Golden Ball Inn, the group had gone in search of the noisiest tavern — the noisiest because those in it must have money to spend, and be drunk already. This guaranteed loose purses and plenty of coins for the jongleurs. Walking down the length of Northgate Street, where every other house seemed to brew and sell its own beer, it had not taken long to find a suitable place. A mob of young men had burst out of a door, collapsing drunkenly at Margaret Peper's pretty feet. A roar of cheering voices followed their passage into the lane from a bright, taper-lit room. One finely dressed youth picked himself up, swept up Margaret's hand, and covered it in kisses. He then attempted a wobbly bow, and stepped back into the open sewer that ran down the centre of the street. His comrades rescued him from his stinking pit and raced off into the dark whooping and cheering.

De Askeles ushered his crew into the nameless tavern, and expertly eyed up the throng of cheery revellers. The low-ceilinged room held a press of bodies clad in bright clothes of red and green and purple, with here and there the more sombre black gown of the academic. There were few tonsured heads, and few young faces, which gave de Askeles cause to smile. Oxford teachers and students alike had few coins to spare, whereas the travelling merchant, away from mistress and home, was often profligate with his earnings. A few flushed faces were turned curiously towards the newcomers, and de Askeles took hold of the opportunity.

'Friends, I come to bring you pleasure.'

His powerful voice carried over the buzz of animated chatter and caused a lull in the noise. Everyone's eyes turned to him. Having caught the whole room's attention, he continued.

'I am Stefano de Askeles, and I bring you a troupe of jongleurs who have performed before kings, and at a private audience with the Pope. Tonight we will perform not for idle nobility, but for you.'

With an expansive gesture, he took in all those in the smoky room. A myriad tallow candles flickered on upturned faces, some disbelieving, some already taken in by de Askeles's silver tongue. He raised his left arm high in the air, and the long, slashed sleeve lined in crimson fell back like a curtain, revealing the slim figure of Margaret Peper.

'I bring you the sinuous Margaretha.'

To gasps of admiration, Margaret bent backwards at her slender waist, placing her hands just behind her feet, and flipped head over heels, landing adroitly in the lap of a red-faced man clad in well-cut robes. He started, then grasped at Margaret's hips, hooting and leering at his companions. De Askeles turned to a group of youths near the door, lifting his right arm.

'And the mysteries of the dextrous Robbio.'

Robert plucked a multi-coloured ball apparently out of the air, then two more from his mouth, and began to juggle with them. The youths burst into wild applause.

'But best of all, may I present the angelic voice of Monsignor Carmina.'

De Askeles waved his arms and Simon Godrich stepped forward, drawing the slender shape of his rebec from a pouch at his side. He sat on a convenient stool and, holding the instrument by its stringed neck, nestled the sounding box in his lap. With the bow in his other hand, he drew a melodious cascade of notes from the strings.

'He has songs of Pilate and Herod, laments of poverty . . .'

There were groans from the attentive throng.

'. . . songs on the vanity of life, and the rewards of faith . . .'

This brought forth more groans and good-humoured catcalls, for they guessed where this list would inevitably end. De Askeles smiled, and gave in.

'. . . or songs of drink, dice-playing and debauchery.'

Wild cheers almost drowned out the beginning of Simon's first song.

* * *

The old man tried to clear his mind of violent thoughts. After all, he had only had a glimpse of the other just now, and it had been a long time since it had all happened. To another it might have seemed a minor incident, but to him it had been a grave insult. Worthy of retribution. Wearily, he tried to put it from his mind and began with incantations to Hermes, prophet, King of Egypt and ancient god of reproduction. If anyone was to reveal the secrets of the fifth essence to him, it would be Hermes. It was said that he received his revelations from an angel of God. But his records of the true method of distilling the quintessence were lost. The alchemist had seen many texts claiming to be the words of the philosopher Hermes, and many times he had been excited by the prospect of achieving the tempting dual goals of eternal youth and the transmutation of base metals into gold. But every time the formulas were proved to have been written by lesser mortals, and none of them had worked.

He passed his hands over his eyes, as though wiping the temptations from his brain. His was a search for pure knowledge, he reminded himself. He rose from in front of the flickering candle he used as a focus for his prayers to Hermes and straightened his aching legs. He grimaced, and thought that the restoration of youth was a seductive idea nevertheless. He was already in his fiftieth year and his limbs protested at the Oxford winter, damp and chilly as it was. However, the furnace would soon warm the crypt-like cellar in which he carried out his clandestine work.

He began to stir the red-hot coals through the little archway cut in the side of the funnel-shaped furnace. The red glow threw his shadow on the low ceiling and walls so that it looked as though a large and menacing bird hovered above his back. He took the candle from his makeshift altar and held it over the array of rare and expensive glass alembics above the mouth of the funnel. The flame glinted off the surface of the glass and turned the fluid contents of the largest globe a soft golden colour. The alchemist took it as a promising sign.

The surface of the liquid began to bubble as the heat from the furnace transferred itself. This part of the creation of the quintessence was familiar to the alchemist. Many times before he had begun with the best Rhenish wine and distilled it seven times to get what the texts called burning water. The requirement then was to distil a further thousand times, though he didn't know if this was a literal truth or not. He screwed up his soft brown eyes and squinted into the long glass tube that ran from the top of the alembic. As the vapour rose from the surface of his burning water it condensed in the greenish tube and little sparkling drops fell from the end into the container he had placed below to catch the precious fluid. Impatient, he crooked his little finger below the tube and caught one of the drops. Transferring it to his mouth, he sucked on the finger and smiled at the fiery taste of the fluid. The first stages had begun.

'Bacchus loves to visit
Always without count,
The wooded slopes and hills
On top of Venus' mount.'

Simon Godrich's clear tones carried the song out on to the street. Like the spume on the crest of a wave, it seemed to ripple on top of the raucous cries of drunken men. Peter Bullock sighed and leaned back in the doorway across from the tavern. He supposed he might have to exercise his club-wielding arm this night, if matters got any further out of hand. Damned jongleurs, they always got people excited with their songs and acrobatic antics. A heady brew taken along with the beer that William Kepeharm sold. Bullock himself would not touch the ale that came out of Kepeharm's spigot. He knew how close his water supply was to the open sewer that ran out into the street.

'Gaudeamus igitur
Juvenes dum sumus.'

The chorus was shouted rather than sung by the assembled gathering inside the tavern. For most it was the only bit of Latin they would ever know, outside of what they heard and rarely understood in church. Bullock eased his hunched back into the angle of the door and its frame, and ran his rough fingers through his tangled grey hair. The night was cold, and a mind-numbing drizzle was turning to sleet. His hair was wet and clung to his forehead; his clothes were wet and chafed uncomfortably against his frozen limbs. He remembered a time when he would have been in the tavern, or one like it, with his comrades-in-arms. He would have been thinking no further than his next drink and the possibility of taking the serving-girl somewhere quiet for some mutual pleasures. Now he resented those out to enjoy themselves, who could ruin a quiet night for a constable. Employed by the burghers of the town to take on their responsibility of maintaining the law, he wished for no more than a peaceful, sober, law-abiding citizenry. In Oxford, and around its walls, this was an impossible dream.

He supposed that in a small measure the town only reflected the unhappy nature of England generally. The fortunate few with money at their disposal huddled together for comfort, taking their fleeting pleasures when they could.

They employed men like himself to lock up the towns against the poor and the vagabonds, in the hope of creating a few islands of safety. The change in fortunes of the King and the unexpected defeat of Earl Simon a couple of years earlier had left the country crawling with dispossessed barons and starving soldiery. He had heard that this very year a group of landless barons had settled themselves on the isle of Ely and were pillaging the surrounding countryside. They had even kidnapped some rich Jews from Norwich and were holding them for ransom. It was all too close for comfort.

For now, he must concentrate on the relatively easy task of keeping some drunken revellers under control. Stirring his stiffening limbs as the winter wind bit through his layers of clothes and drove the sleet at him afresh, he regretted his advancing years and wished he were indoors.

* * *

Tucked warmly in a corner of the tavern, Stefano de Askeles was mining information from the rich deposits of idle chatter around him. Already he had learned that the Prior of St Frideswide was eager to mount a religious drama to cap the success of his miraculous blessing of the saint's limbs a few days earlier. The troupe's offer of its services must have been very timely. Now he was learning of an envious priest who desired some relics for himself in order to attract pilgrims of his own. The fat merchant in whose lap Margaret had first landed furnished him with all he needed to know.

'Petysance is a fool. I mean, who has heard of St Aldate, and what sort of miracles would his bones perform if they existed? It would truly be a miracle if they could be found at all.'

Even as he spoke, his eyes were glued to the spinning form of Margaret Peper, who was executing a perfect cartwheel in the confined space between the tables. His cronies pounded their fists in pleasure on the battered table around which they sat, causing a tankard of ale to bounce off and scatter its contents across the already slimy floor. De Askeles laughed with them, but behind the mask of merriment his mind was already working on a plan to furnish Edward Petysance with his heart's desire. His own training as a youth had furnished him with enough knowledge of the saints — major and minor — to be able successfully to swindle priests eager for relics.

Margaret, her acrobatics completed, slumped next to the leader of the troupe. Holding a smile on her lips, she asked when they would be free of this lecherous crowd.

'My thighs are black and blue from unwanted gropings. Haven't they seen a woman's legs before?'

'Not as pretty as yours. Their wives probably have shanks like draft horses.'

Margaret rubbed the mess of ale-soaked rushes from her hands and forced a wider smile to her lips as the fat merchant squeezed her thighs yet again. De Askeles gently weighed the bag of coins he now held in his hand, and estimated that their work was done for the night. Besides, the sweet odours of the perspiring saltatore at his side was rousing his own passions. He slid his free hand to her much abused thigh and felt the animal warmth exuding from it. He also felt Margaret's body tighten under his hand.

She wondered if this were the moment and her hand slipped behind her back to grasp the weapon Godrich had passed on to her that evening. It was the implement the robber had dropped — not a knife but some sort of workman's tool. She had begged it from Simon as a means of self-defence, never really admitting to herself whom she actually wanted to use it against till now. Now she knew she could kill him. As if guessing what she proposed to do, de Askeles pushed his body hard against hers and trapped her hand behind her back. The moment was gone and she submitted to his overpowering strength of will. Stefano smiled. Tonight John Peper would have to be entrusted with an urgent errand that kept him away from his wife.

* * *

Peter Bullock returned to Kepeharm's inn after a brisk walk around the perimeter of the city. He had encountered little more than a youth vomiting his meagre supper into the dunghill at the rear of St Aldate's Church. The constable could not quibble at such considerate voidance and left him to his misery. He sighed as he turned towards North Gate to encounter the cries of drunken revelry still emanating from the tavern he had left some time ago. He had hoped that matters would quieten down during his patrol, and not require him to act. As he propelled his hunchbacked body towards the seat of the noise, he saw a shadowy figure emerging from the narrow lane halfway along the street. Whoever it was did not see the constable, for he turned abruptly away from him and slunk towards the locked city gate. Bullock stopped and sought to hide his not inconsiderable frame in the nearest doorway. The man's furtive actions required some discreet observation. He might even be an accomplice of the robbers that plagued the countryside around, intent on letting them into the city. Peering round the shabby lintel, he saw, however, that the figure had stopped outside the still noisy tavern and was peering in at the window arch. The light from inside played briefly on the face and revealed a man with long dark hair and lean features. Whatever he saw caused him considerable anguish, for he angrily punched the rough daub wall of the tavern and averted his gaze. Bullock pulled back into the shallow doorway as the man's face turned towards him.

* * *

Angry at being left with Will to secure their possessions and guard the wagon, John Peper waited until de Askeles, his wife and the others had gone in search of an audience, then hurriedly completed his tasks. He was fearful of what might happen between Margaret and de Askeles, indeed what had probably already happened. He knew he had only been left behind in order to give de Askeles an opportunity to paw his wife. He knew she had only married him because of his usefulness to her — he was adept at getting money out of people who stopped to watch her perform — and had no illusions about his own skills as a troubadour. But still she was his wife and he loved her in his own way. Now he seemed to be losing her to that shallow boaster de Askeles. He resolved to take some action immediately. He gave Will Plome the soft leather collar with a small metal loop attached that he had fashioned from an old jerkin.

'Here, put this on Ham. And don't worry, it will be all right. The leather is soft and will not hurt him. As for Stefano, the animal has probably had greater frights from wild beasts in its own land than it got from him today.'

Will took the collar glumly, turning it over in his great fists, and went off towards the wagon. John decided he could leave the youth in charge and slip away. Will Plome might be simple, but he was quite capable of ensuring no one stole anything from them. Peper therefore hurried over his own repast and made haste to prepare the root vegetables to feed Ham. The animal had been a lucky gambling win of de Askeles's, otherwise he would never have had enough money to purchase such a rare creature, said to have come from the Afric lands in the possession of a returning crusader. Because of its origin, de Askeles had named it Ham in remembrance of one of Noah's sons and his inheritance of that portion of the world. However, he clearly did not comprehend the true value of the creature, for he provided it with the meanest of provender.

Peper went over to the wagon and passed the wooden bowl of blackened turnip and shrivelled apples to Will, who thrust it through the bars of Ham's cage, almost embarrassed at the offering. The monkey's black face with its white cheek tufts peered out at him, its eyes open wide and trusting. It seemed to care not a jot about the poor food and chittered happily as it picked delicately through the fare as though it were the richest meal at the most princely of tables. John turned his attention to the simpleton, telling him to put the collar he was still holding reluctantly in his hand on Ham before de Askeles returned. Giving him the most strict of instructions not to leave the courtyard, and to challenge anyone who approached the wagon, Peper was at last able to seek to spy on de Askeles and his wife.

He spent a fruitless time poking his head in the doorways of innumerable taverns and failing to discover the whereabouts of the rest of the troupe. Finally, he ran into a band of raucous students in the narrow lane behind St Mary's Church who were exchanging lascivious rejoinders about the 'prettiest saltatore in Christendom'. Their description of her back somersault and where it might be expected to end lay in the realms of the fanciful, but Peper knew they must be referring to Margaret. As they jostled him and winked at each other, he managed to elicit the location of the tavern where she and her comrades were performing. Leaving the students to their lecherous imaginings, he scuttled down the narrow alley that ran to the north of the High Street. He did not want to attract the attention of any watchman, who might take him for a night-walker intent on robbery. Unfortunately, his clandestine behaviour only served to achieve the effect he sought to avoid. His was the mystery figure Peter Bullock observed.

He stepped cautiously out of the end of the lane and on to the street leading to North Gate. The riotous noise from the tavern to his right drew his notice, and he did not see Peter Bullock squeezing his bent body into the darkness further down the street. Sneaking up close to the window nearest him, he peered through the torn sacking that hung in the unglazed frame. His gaze was drawn inexorably to the slim figure of his wife, her face glowing red from her exertions, and the imposing form of de Askeles next to her. His hand was placed conspicuously on her thigh.

John Peper tore his gaze away from the painful sight and punched the wall. He swore he would kill the man as soon as the opportunity presented itself.

CHAPTER FOUR

GOD: For I must wend a path to trace
To set this bliss in every tower
Each one of you will keep his place
And Lucifer, I make thee governor.

The Fall of Lucifer

With the appearance of the messenger at the Chancellor's lodgings, Thomas de Cantilupe knew that his gamble had begun to pay off. At first he had been full of anger when he was awoken by the insistent tugging on the sleeve of his hair shirt. He had consumed an enormous quantity of the present Chancellor's best Poitou the previous evening and did not expect to be roused so early. And certainly not before the sun had risen. A greyish dawn was barely sneaking through the shutters of the bedchamber, and there was that nuisance Halegod insisting he awaken. He pulled his arm back into the warmth under the coverlet and felt the first admonitory prickle of the rough hair shirt he wore night and day in penance for sins and excesses past and future. But Halegod's persistent nagging continued unabated.

'Master, there's a messenger says he must speak to the Chancellor immediately.'

'Then tell him to get on his way to Southampton, and to stop disturbing the innocent.'

De Cantilupe's reply was muffled by the covers he had pulled over his head. After a few moments' silence, he assumed the servant had left and poked a bleary eye over the top of the bedclothes. Halegod was still hovering over his bed, his face framed by the early morning sun filtering through his wispy hair. It stood out like a halo around his head. Even in shadow, de Cantilupe detected a smug grin on his antique features. He groaned.

'There is more to tell, is there not?'

'Not if you wish me to send the King's messenger on his way.'

With that parting shot, the old man left the ex-Chancellor's bedroom.

'The King . . . ?'

At the all-important word, the former Chancellor of Oxford and of England sat up abruptly and swung his bare legs off the bed. The informant at the King's court who had told de Cantilupe that Henry planned to spend Christmas in Oxford that year had been correct. And de Cantilupe's forged message to de Cicestre, telling of the serious illness of his aged mother, had successfully cleared the way for him. He splashed his face with the icy water from the bowl that Halegod had thoughtfully placed by his bedside, then went to call the old man to bring his clothes. Halegod already stood in the doorway with suitable attire to meet the messenger — de Cantilupe had forgotten how infuriatingly good a servant the old man was.

So without too much delay de Cantilupe found himself clad in a sombre brown robe with a fur-trimmed collar to drive away the winter chills, and ready to receive the message to the Chancellor from the King. What could be more natural, since he was present in Oxford when the incumbent appeared to be God-knows-where, than to act on the contents of the message, and prove his undying loyalty to the King?

'Now Heaven and Earth is made by me,
The earthly void is all I see,
At my bidding is made the light,
Divided from the blackest night.
Great torches I shall make two,
Both the sun and moon also.
Stars I make upon the firmament,
The Earth to light is mine intent.
Now this is done all at my bidding,
Beasts go crawling, flying, swimming,
And all my works to my liking
I do now find.'

De Askeles's rich voice rose into the quiet void of the priory church of St Frideswide. It seemed to ascend on wings to the highest rafters of the lofty wooden ceiling, then echo off the dressed stone walls of nave and chancel. It was so compelling that the Prior could almost believe it truly was the word of God booming out. However, he had to bring himself back to earth — he could not allow the troupe of jongleurs to perform inside the church anymore. The bishop had expressly forbidden it since novice monks had been led to perform more secular interludes in counterpoint to the edifying dramatization of the liturgy. Interludes sometimes of doubtful rectitude. Regretfully, he took the leader of the troupe, who had performed so mightily as God, to the imposing south-west entrance of the church and out into the chilly morning air. But de Askeles was not going to give up so easily — he knew the priest would do almost anything to have the mystery plays presented. The inside of the church was no longer acceptable, and the back of his wagon was not grand enough for a site of such potential. There only remained one other possibility, and he raised it. Their breath came in great spouts of steam as they discussed the option of raising a stage in the open, using the massive church doors as a backdrop.

'What more appropriate as the doors of heaven?' wheedled the heavy-built de Askeles, throwing his long blond locks back with a flick of his hand. The Prior had to admit the prospect was tempting, and after but a moment's thought agreed.

'Very well. But I must see the whole of the text you propose to use.'

'Of course — you have nothing to fear there. I have translated it myself from the French, where it is known as the *"Passion des Jongleurs"*. A truly Christian epic starting with the Creation . . .'

Here de Askeles waved his hand to indicate the performance he had given inside the church.

'. . . including the fall of Lucifer and Adam, and concluding with the Final Judgement. But of course the centrepiece is Christ's Passion and Ascension.'

The Prior nodded in approval at de Askeles's reverent tones.

'Still, I would see the text.'

De Askeles bowed extravagantly, and produced a sheaf of bound papers from a pouch at his side. He had anticipated the cleric's request and had prepared this copy for his perusal. There was nothing in it to which the Prior could object, especially as it did not contain the whole text. Once in performance it would be impossible for the cleric to raise any objections. The Prior took the text and shook the actor's hand. De Askeles made to leave, and then, as though having a sudden, further thought, he turned back to the Prior, a sad frown on his noble face.

'There is the matter of constructing the stage. It must be sturdy, and with trapdoors to enable us to present the Harrowing of Hell . . .'

He left the statement unfinished, and the Prior realized he would have to fund the *representatio* if it were to happen at all. Well, nothing came for nothing, and the King was in

Oxford and may be persuaded to attend. The expense would be worth it *and* the wood could be re-used afterwards, no doubt.

'I will talk to my bursar. He will furnish the requisite funds and can employ carpenters from the town guild to erect it.'

De Askeles performed another of his extravagant bows, hiding a smirk of triumph as he cast his gaze to the ground. He too was thinking of the King's presence in Oxford. This Christmas could be very profitable for him indeed. His pleasure so emboldened him that he dared to raise a personal matter, but one that he assured the Prior was of great religious importance, concerning necromancy.

* * *

The servants at the King's palace at Beaumont scuttled back and forth in a fever of tidying. The King, Queen Eleanor, the Papal Legate and innumerable nobles had finally arrived at Oxford the previous evening, and Henry had tumbled straight into his bed. This morning he had arisen early and let everyone know that he was dissatisfied. Despite approaching his sixtieth year, Henry stormed vigorously about the place insisting that the contents of the huge baggage train that followed his perambulations around the country be sorted immediately and arranged in the rooms of the palace. The familiar furniture made him feel as though he lived permanently within these walls, as it did in every temporary residence he occupied. At his age, familiarity was a comforting feeling.

Tired functionaries had not carried out this task last night, and now harassed menservants manoeuvred massive oaken chairs and tables into position, while precious tapestries were carefully unfolded and draped strategically in the great hall and the King's bedchamber to prevent the draughts to which his ageing body was increasingly susceptible. The hierarchy of servants, from marshal through yeoman usher and wardrober right down to groom, hurried to the tasks they had carried out a hundred times before in as many different places. The King's presence, with his enormous household, was too great a drain on the resources of any one community for him to stay too long. Moving from place to place was a prerequisite of the court's survival. Already the steward, the controller and the clerk of the kitchen would be ordering the delivery of mountains of food for the King's Christmas banquet as well as the daily needs of his entourage, for although the day-to-day administration of the kingdom was carried out by clerks who stayed in Westminster, the big decisions were taken by the King and his court on the road. Taxes were also collected locally in cash or kind, and that also required skilled clerks. After fifty years as monarch, however, Henry had become insensible of all this industry, and when one tiny part of it failed, he lost his temper.

The King's anger today was also fuelled by the refusal of the Earl of Gloucester to attend his Christmas revels. The earl was still sulking about a disagreement with Roger Mortimer over the disinherited barons. Gloucester had proposed that the barons could reclaim their lands, lost when they supported de Montfort, by paying a ransom to the King. In this way a band of disgruntled lords who were ravaging the countryside, having nothing more to lose, could be brought under control. Mortimer objected, mainly because he had personally benefited from the barons' disinheritance. He would have to return lands he now controlled. Henry had hoped to reconcile the two men over a Christmas banquet, but now Gloucester had spoiled his plans. How could he restore order to his kingdom if his nobles could not agree amongst themselves?

Also, he was only now getting reports that the citizens of Lynn had failed him. They had petitioned him to restore their liberties, lost after the Barons' War, if they succeeded in rounding up the young de Montfort whelps, Thomas de Crespigny and the rest on Ely. Apparently, the rag-tag army of Lynn had been fooled into thinking the knights had fled, and had walked into an ambush. Now there were more deaths to avenge. He knew in the end he would have to deal with the disinherited himself.

The final straw had come yesterday, when a band of ragged brigands had had the temerity to attack his wagon train south of Oxford. The King's own wagon train! It was true they had been easily beaten off by his personal bodyguard, but it simply should not have happened. He had woken at dawn shaking in anger and despatched a frightened messenger to Oxford to summon the Chancellor and town burghers. Now he paced up and down in his solar pulling his grey and straggly bifurcated beard with both hands. A frown creased his already wrinkled face as he impatiently awaited the arrival of the Oxford worthies. His servants knew well to keep out of his way when the King was in this mood. At such times they were glad to be mere servants and not prominent citizens whom the King could take to task for real and imagined slights alike.

De Cantilupe, on the other hand, knew the risks associated with high office and revelled in the dangers associated with staying at the top of the heap. He strode out at the head of the motley crew of merchants and landowners summoned to the King. Fear and panic might have been etched on their faces, but a smile of anticipation covered his. The group left the city confines through the North Gate, passing under the Bocardo prison that crowned the gate's arch. The King's residence was outside the city walls, for it was said that any monarch entering Oxford did so at his own peril, bringing the wrath of the Virgin down on him. The last time Henry himself had incautiously ridden through the gates, he had gone on to nearly lose his kingdom to Simon de Montfort. He was now a more temperate man.

Beyond the North Gate were the ramshackle dwellings of Beaumont, lining the approach to the King's palace. The stinking hovels leaned one against the other, as though each depended on its neighbour for support. Pigs rooted indiscriminately outside the houses and in, churning up dirt floors with their sensitive snouts. Snotty children sat in the midst of this midden, unattended by their mothers, who no doubt still slept after the night's exertions. De Cantilupe thought it ironic that the King's residence was surrounded by those of thieves and whores. Some said the King likewise surrounded himself at court with similar creatures, albeit ostensibly of nobler ancestry.

Oxford's most prominent citizens were led into the great hall of the King's palace and abandoned. Some of them had been in this place before, but it still awed them. The lofty roof beams arched up into a Stygian gloom from which descended the banners of the King and his favoured nobles. The fact that their gilded opulence was obscured by a heavy layer of dust did not diminish their intimidating effect; it only served to emphasize the seeming permanence of those who ruled England. Fortunes might have shifted from one family to another in recent years, but the baton of power was always handed around the same small group.

In the safety of his own home, each merchant present might rail against the chaos abroad in the kingdom, and intimate poor governance. In the supportive embrace of his guild colleagues, he might imagine that his decisions actually controlled the day-to-day affairs of England. But in the presence of naked power, he quaked with fear like the rudest peasant.

De Cantilupe was not afraid — after all he had played the same game himself with supplicants at court when he had been Chancellor. He knew the King would delay his entrance until he had made the merchants sweat, and then sweep through the massive double doors at the head of the hall. Separating himself from the huddle of tradesmen, he drifted towards that end of the hall and stood in a shaft of morning light that pierced the darkness. In this way, the King would be sure to see and recognize him.

Time passed. Just when even de Cantilupe was thinking the King had forgotten about them, the doors near where he stood did indeed crash open as he had predicted. Henry's position at the head of a flight of steps allowed him to dominate the company, even though his frame was slight and stooped with age. He stood in the archway, his gnarled hands hidden in gloves of the softest Roman leather. Thumbs thrust into his belt, he looked down at the assembled merchants as though they were naughty children. As his gaze passed over them, a flicker of recognition seemed to register at the sight of de Cantilupe: It was difficult for the former Chancellor to be sure, though, at the King's left eyelid had a droop that often made Henry appear to be winking at his audience.

When he spoke, the King's voice was powerful despite his years.

'It had already come to my ears that there was no district more infamous than this for the committing of the crimes of robbery and murder. But it appears these crimes are not sufficient. No, my own wagon train has been despoiled and barrels of wine removed. My very person was in danger only last evening.'

There was a hubbub of protestations of outrage from those assembled, but Henry cut through it with a voice trembling with anger.

'I believe there is a conspiracy here between the robbers and my own appointed justiciars. And in the circumstances this amounts to treason.'

The final word fell like a hammer blow on the already battered brows of those present. Their faces went chalky-white — some of them were indeed the King's appointed justiciars — but protestations of innocence were stifled in arid throats. De Cantilupe knew he had to think quickly, or he would be included in Henry's indiscriminate anger. He cursed his morning's eagerness to present himself to the King.

* * *

Stefano de Askeles was well pleased with his progress towards the mounting of his play. At terce, he had persuaded the Prior of St Frideswide of the necessity to construct a stage, and by the middle of the day the area in front of the church's imposing doors was a maelstrom of activity. Carpenters ran hither and thither with great balks of timber, and the air rang with the thud of nails and pegs being driven into beech and solid oak. Having dictated where the trapdoor should be for the descent into hell, de Askeles left John Peper in charge of raising the framework at the rear of the platform from which would hang their precious painted depictions of the Temple, Jerusalem, Nazareth and the Celestial Paradise. Now he strutted around the wooden stage, wearing his favourite Devil's mask. Two immense, curved ram's horns curled out from the top of the mask, which was painted black. Red-rimmed eyes stared out of massive white pools almost filling the top half of the face. The Devil's nose was no more than a button compressed between those staring eyes and the great gash of a mouth. The Evil One's maw was wide open and filled with serrated rows of ugly needle-like teeth, and at the back of the throat a forked tongue flickered as de Askeles shook his head. His golden locks were completely hidden by the mask, which fitted like a helmet, and was held in place by cords that tied the horn-heavy effigy to his skull. He wore it because it made him feel powerful.

Peper had been curt with him that morning, but he could not be bothered to cut the man down to size. Time enough for that later when he had spoken to the priest of St Aldate's, Edward Petysance. In the meanwhile Peper had better ensure the carpenters worked hard, for they had precious little time. As he bent to jump down from the developing stage, he spotted a man laying down his tools and taking a jug up from the earth. The carpenter had already come to de Askeles's attention as he often stopped work to share a joke with his comrades. His shock of red hair made him stand out, as did his arrogant behaviour, standing in the midst of the other men with hands on hips. He had heard the man's name, Ralph, being called out from one end of the site to the other, and he meant to squash him as an example to the others to get on with their work.

Ralph now squatted down on his haunches below the stage, and tipped his head back, drinking greedily from the jug. Swiftly de Askeles crossed the stage and, swinging his booted foot viciously, kicked the jug from the thirsty man's lips. Ralph cried out in surprise and looked in astonishment as the ale jug flew out of his hands and shattered against a pile of timbers. Wrenching his head round to see who had done this to him, he looked up to see the face of the Devil staring down at him. For a moment he was frozen with fear, then the figure above him lifted the mask away to reveal the ferocious visage of the leader of the jongleurs, his mane of golden hair framing his angry face. Ralph clenched his fists at his side and stood in silence as the man berated him for his laziness. Only when the jongleur stormed off did the carpenter stare at his retreating back and promise revenge.

De Askeles was unaware of the anger he had caused, and the shaking fist with which he was threatened. His mind was now on Petysance and his desire for a holy relic. He already had some ideas how he could furnish the man with what he needed. With the remains of St Frideswide setting the standard, nothing less than a saintly skeleton would be required.

CHAPTER FIVE

LUCIFER: Distress! I command you now to cease
And see the beauty I bear;
All Heaven shines through me alone
God himself shines never so clear.

The Fall of Lucifer

At the heart of Oxford lay the substantial stone-built houses of Jewry. Tucked securely between the confines of the priory church of St Frideswide, and the churches of All Saints and St Mary's on the city's main thoroughfare, Jewry was a network of narrow lanes and back-to-back houses that offered mutual protection to the Jews of Oxford. They were tolerated in England because of their trade, the only trade they were allowed to ply — that of usury. Christians were forbidden to make money by lending money, but the overlords of the Christian world survived by borrowing when they required it. The King had the privilege of levying taxes should he need money. The barons relied on borrowed coin.

But Falconer was not in Jewry to borrow. He knew and respected the Jews in Oxford, not for the moneylending but for their scholarship. His oldest friend in Jewry was the Rabbi Jehozadok, who lived surrounded by books in the Scola Judaeorum. Of late the old man's eyes had dimmed with a chalky cast, covering what before had been a piercing gaze. Falconer had taken to visiting him in the evening and, under the pretext of doing his own reading, read aloud to the old sage. In this way, he kept Jehozadok in touch with that which kept him alive. Scholarship.

Now Falconer hurried to consult him in the daytime, unable to suppress his curiosity until the usual evening appointment. Jehozadok's partial blindness did not prevent him from being unusually aware of everything that went on around him. Indeed, his affliction probably aided his knowledge of activity across the scholarly city, for many people made a point of dropping in on the old man to ensure his poor sight did not cut him off from the world. Each one brought a titbit of news like busy starlings feeding their young, flitting between the outside world and the security of the nest. Without leaving the Scola, Jehozadok gathered more information than any one of his able-bodied feeders. Now Falconer wished to mine that knowledge in his search for the alchemist Friar Bacon had referred to in his letter.

Before he was even in sight of St Frideswide's Church, he was aware of the sound of feverish activity. The rasp of timbers being cut, and the thump of hammers driving home nails, forewarned him of the preparations that were being made for the presentation of the annual Christmas plays at the church. As he passed the western end, he could see the massive platform on which a horde of workmen toiled, like ants around the queen's nest. This year looked as though it was going to be a special year. He had already heard that some travelling players were in Oxford — perhaps they would raise the level of the plays' presentation from that of amateur enthusiasm in the hands of the monks, merchants and priests to something worth seeing.

Two men struggled to raise a painted cloth on a row of posts, and the chill air caused their laboured breath to steam from their lips. Falconer caught a glimpse of painted trees, unseasonably green, surrounding an edifice outlined in gold. The gilded edging sparkled in the watery sun, then the image was turned away from him to face out into the courtyard. The back of the cloth had a greyish, tantalizing mirror image of that which had attracted his attention. He was left wondering if the building he had glimpsed was the House of Bishops or the Temple. He would have to ensure he carried his eye-lenses with him when he watched the presentation. Treading carefully over the icy slush that filled the rutted lane, he threaded his way down the narrow wynd that led to the Scola.

* * *

People came to the alchemist for cures for many ills because they knew of his uncommon understanding of the mysteries of judicial astronomy, which some called astrology. The alchemist preferred the former phrase, and relegated the word astrology to purely speculative studies of the stars. The use of speculative astrology stunk of magic and fixed prediction of the future. A true astronomer only predicted events conditionally and drew attention to man's free will to change matters. Of course the only people he deigned to advise were those of some importance in the city. The poor and ill could be left to the common apothecaries and leeches that were numerous in Oxford.

The nervous man in front of him now was a burgher of the merchants' guild, who had strangely refused his offer of a seat. He stood before the alchemist hopping from one neatly clad foot to the other, as the scholar lifted down a heavy, leather-bound tome from a shelf at his side. He laid it on the table between himself and the agitated patient and opened it at a well-thumbed page. On the page was the outline of a naked man with wild hair and a full, bifurcated beard. The figure was surrounded with scribbled writings and the alchemist peered closely at them, attempting to decipher their meaning.

'You say you are born under the sign of Scorpio?'

'Indeed.'

'Then it is your bladder about which you are complaining?'

The skinny merchant marvelled at the alchemist's precise understanding of his problem. The alchemist merely waved away the other's admiration with a flick of his hand.

'A medical man must of necessity know the nature and conjunction of the stars, and this reference' — he pointed at the sketch of the naked man before him on the table — 'confirms that a Scorpio must beware of cutting of the buttocks and the arse, and of hurting of the bladder.'

'And is there a cure?' asked the uncomfortable merchant, who was already casting a nervous glance over his shoulder in search of the nearest place where he could relieve himself.

'There is a cure recommended by my old friend Friar Bacon. It is compounded of precious pearl that has been exposed to your star's influence for eight days and nights.'

He paused.

'It is rather costly, mind you.'

The agitated merchant reached for his purse, for he was in considerable discomfort. Never mind the cost of the cure, he simply sought relief, and after all more coin could easily be earned. The alchemist shuffled out of the room, and shortly returned with a tiny, stoppered vial made of glass. He held it reverently before the merchant, whose hungry eyes feasted on the fluid that sparkled inside the container. He eagerly slipped the silver coins into the alchemist's outstretched hand and took the vial in return. The alchemist ushered him out, closing the door on his elaborate protestations of gratitude. Returning to the reception room he cast aside the book of remedies with which he had impressed the merchant as though it were nothing.

Indeed he considered it so, compared to what he had safely hidden in the small chest below the table. With trembling hands he stooped down and pushed a key into the lock. It turned easily, for he often had recourse to the contents of the chest in his pursuit of knowledge. He lifted the metal-banded lid, and reverently removed a cloth bundle from its resting place. Placing it gently on the table before him, he unfolded the wrapping. No matter how many times he revealed the contents of the bundle, he was always struck dumb by it. It was a book, the pages yellowed and fragile with age. He carefully opened it at the point where he had last inserted a piece of red ribbon as a marker, and began to decipher the text.

* * *

As William Falconer began his hunt for Friar Bacon's alchemist friend, Thomas de Cantilupe was planning how to get himself out of a fix. The King, recognizing his former colleague, had temporarily released him from the imprisonment in which he had placed the burghers of Oxford. The King had vowed that he would clear the countryside of the vagrant robbers that infested it. Whether or not he truly believed that the burghers knew of, or were acting in concert with, the brigands, was not clear to de Cantilupe. What was indisputable was that Henry had threatened to hang the imprisoned good men of Oxford, including de Cantilupe. The former Chancellor had been released to round up men who would name the conspirators. His problem was convincing anyone else to venture into the old lion's lair, where they might share the fate of their predecessors.

De Cantilupe shivered and clutched his robes around him. The Chancellor's rooms were cold, and the lazy Halegod had not lit a fire. Perhaps he had thought that de Cantilupe would be warmly wrapped in the favour of the King by now. He certainly would have been only a few years ago, but times had changed and Henry was more cautious. He stuck his head into the icy passage leading to the servants' quarters and called the old man's name. There was no response, not even the shuffle of the soft shoes the old man habitually wore. Either the fool was deaf, or he was deliberately ignoring the former Chancellor. Something else he would not have had to suffer a few years back, when he was at the height of his power.

He called Halegod again, but all he heard was the echo of his own voice. He was alone in the house. He had a mind to tell the King that the old man was the outlaws' go-between, who ensured the city burghers turned a blind eye to the robbers' misdeeds. That would repay him for his insolence. He stomped back into Henry de Cicestre's main room, and kicked at the forlorn ashes in the hearth. Then suddenly the thought of revenging himself on Halegod blossomed into a solution to his problems. Most merchants had some business rival they envied, someone who had beaten them to a profitable deal, or some handsome youth who had cuckolded them. Perhaps even the good Prior of St Frideswide's had a few names he could supply. If they were prepared to accompany him into the presence of the King, they could denounce whomsoever they chose. And the King would conveniently dispose of them in the name of ridding the neighbourhood of the brigands and their cronies. Of course, the fact that it would also save de Cantilupe's neck was of even greater importance. Why, he could even settle some old scores for himself. What was the name of that regent master who had been a thorn in his flesh through all his years as Chancellor of the university? Called after a bird, wasn't he? The name came suddenly to his lips.

'William Falconer.'

* * *

'William, old friend. Come and sit beside me.'

The old man motioned with his gnarled hand to indicate that Falconer should not stand on ceremony but join him at the hearthside where blazed and crackled a warming fire. Jehozadok's other hand rested on the open pages of a book, as though it gave him comfort to feel the smooth surface and the rough tracks of the scribe's pen that covered it. The hand trembled slightly, suggesting a lack of control by the ageing teacher. His cloudy eyes sought to make out the shape of the heavily built regent master as he crossed the room. Falconer knew Jehozadok could no longer see anything more than the outline of those who visited him and marvelled at his ability to name each one. He shuddered at the thought of his own mind being trapped in an ageing and rebellious body.

'As sharp as ever, I see.' His cheery comment belied his real feelings.

'I may not be able to see so well, but the fusty odour of your robes cannot escape my nostrils. Really, William, you should pay more attention to your appearance.'

Falconer blushed but had to admit that he had thrown on the black robe he habitually wore for weeks on end. But what reason had he to wear anything more appealing? His mind returned briefly to the woman who had filled his days some while ago. They had met when Falconer had been investigating one of the murders he became so often obsessed with. Her husband had been one of his main suspects. Using his deductive powers, and with the aid of Aristotelian logic, he had found the real murderer and exonerated the husband, but not before he had been consumed with desire for the wife. Fool that he was, he had even saved the husband's life. Now he dared not so much as say the woman's name for fear of shattering his resolve to avoid her. The liaison was doubly impossible: she was married, and his continuing existence as a regent master teaching at Oxford depended on his remaining unmarried. The logic was incontrovertible, and he sighed hopelessly.

'You have clearly not come to read to me so early in the day. And you obviously have something on your mind. More than one thing, I would imagine.'

Once again the sharpness of the old man's mind belied the appearance of his failing body. Falconer looked around the room in order to compose his thoughts. Jehozadok was surrounded by scholarship — every shelf, every table, indeed every surface was piled high with books, papers and scrolls. The light that filtered in through the unshuttered windows shone like a beacon on the profusion of learning. Sunlight danced on the motes of dust that hovered in the room — a sight that Falconer always associated with his old friend. No text lay still long enough to gather dust as Jehozadok reacquainted himself with its contents.

'I see best when the sun shines.'

The rabbi's statement was ambiguous, and Falconer sought to penetrate the mind behind the milky eyes. He had never been able to truly fathom the depth and scope of the old man's wisdom, which was why he was here now. He would try to shine some light on his difficulty.

'I am seeking an alchemist.'

* * *

The scientist-alchemist sat poised over the treasure like some great insect, his long and scrawny limbs bent double as he peered closely at the words before him. It was said that Aristotle had hidden elusive meanings in the text of his *Secretum Secretorum* and the old man was determined to fathom them out. This translation had been given to him by his old friend Friar Roger Bacon, and was directly from the Arabic by Philip of Tripoli. The friar had left him a copy of the manuscript when he had got wind of his impending incarceration in France. Since then, the alchemist had wished Bacon was available to assist his research, for some matters eluded him and he realized the manuscript was incomplete. The Secret of Secrets hinted of a universal science that brought together all the sciences known to man — astronomy, astrology, mathematics, medicine — everything.

He understood the friar when he spoke of the difference between speculative alchemy and the practical alchemy of experiment. Bacon had only reinforced his reputation as a magician by causing eruptions, strange noises and bright lights in his chamber almost every night of his time in Oxford. The alchemist knew he experimented with methods for turning base metals not into gold, but into far more useful elements.

He had sought a means of making iron of an impenetrable hardness that any armourer would covet. However, the friar had been careless of his dangerous reputation, and it was inevitable that his order should have banished him from England, and forbidden him to practise his black arts. The alchemist was determined not to make a similar mistake, and ensured no one knew of his experiments, especially on the quintessence. His good character as a medical man had once been blemished with suspicions of necromancy, and he did not want it to happen again.

Impatiently, he raised his weary eyes from the Aristotle before him, put it to one side, and drew a more familiar text across the table. It was Bacon's own *De retardatione accidentum senectutis* — a Cure of Old Age and the Preservation of Youth. He felt sure the quintessence would be the ultimate goal of his studies in this area, and his aching limbs urged him to solve the riddle before his body had no youth left in it to preserve.

* * *

The long stretch of the main rostrum before the church of St Frideswide was nearing completion as dusk fell, but the rapid approach of Christmastide demanded that the acting troupe not waste a moment. Even as the carpenters' boy swept away the wood shavings with his hazel besom, Stefano de Askeles strode across the bare boards directing the novice monks of the priory in the location of several blazing torches. The flickering light from their flames cast a magical glow over the painted backdrop, turning the flat scene into something that hovered between heaven and earth. The roar of the flames added its own sense of unreality to the proceedings. De Askeles almost wished he could present all the plays in this half-light, but tradition demanded he at least start the plays in the brightness of the day. Well, he could play out his own fantasies as they rehearsed tonight.

He smoothed the heavy robes he wore in his main role so the white cloth with its multi-coloured edging hung in even folds on his imposing frame and peered imperiously into the gathering gloom beyond the stage. A few of the carpenters, novices and other hangers-on lingered in the courtyard in the hope of seeing the actors perform without paying their few pennies later. De Askeles did not mind this impromptu audience. They were always easily impressed and quickly spread the word that the play-actors were worth seeing. A shuffling of feet behind him reminded him of the task ahead — one he always hated. He turned to face a nervous group of monks and artisans, who had volunteered or been coerced into playing the minor roles in the scenes that were to be enacted. Amongst them was an older monk, Brother Adam, an obsequious but prying soul who de Askeles was convinced had been put there as the Prior's spy. Never mind, he would need them all. Where the Creation of Man only required Adam, Eve, God and the Devil, the Slaying of the Innocents demanded soldiers, women and children, and Christ's Passion and the Ascension, Jews and angels in numbers beyond the capabilities of de Askeles's small troupe. He had therefore to depend on amateurs.

With a sinking heart he motioned for John Peper to distribute the sheets. Some sheets simply bore instructions on where to stand, and these were handed to the artisans — they would not be asked to speak. The other sheets were given to the monks — they contained the few parts that required the actor to say a word or two. Better that the monks played those — at least they could be relied on to be able to read accurately. With a few curt words and a wave of the hand, he selected the older artisans for the soldiers' parts. The younger ones, and a novice monk with a smooth face, he designated as women, much to the amusement of the rest. There were whoops and raucous whistles as one youth primped and preened himself like a common whore in Beaumont. De Askeles didn't know whether his patience would last the night. But he did have plans for Brother Adam.

* * *

Falconer's time with Jehozadok had proved frustrating. The old man had considered all he knew of the philosophical community in Oxford, and shared his knowledge with the regent master. Both knew of the little tutor who carried out dissections of human bodies in his lust to understand the workings of man. Both knew why what he did was a deadly secret. For many years such mutilation of the human body had been expressly forbidden by various popes. But he was not an alchemist. Within Jehozadok's own community there were several medical experts whose comprehension of the use of herbs and other natural resources was vast. Yet none was even rumoured to have an interest in what so many saw as esoteric or, even worse, devilish arts. The rabbi's wrinkled brow was even more furrowed in distraction that he could not assist his friend with the search he had been set.

Falconer took Friar Bacon's letters out of his pouch, unfolded the one addressed to him again and, holding the sealed one as though it were a hot coal, reread the cryptic clue.

'"*No need to go as far as Germany to find this man. Just seek his name from Omega to Alpha.*" What can it mean?'

Jehozadok shook his head.

'Perhaps you should search more closely amongst your mutual friends, or the friar's Franciscan colleagues. It is often those closest to us who surprise us most with their secret interests. That is all I can offer you. But I will continue to think it over and ask amongst those who visit me.'

Falconer shook the weak and shaky hand that was offered him and took his leave. The evening was cold and the slushy furrows in the lane had frozen into awkward ridges that caused Falconer to dance from one foot on to the other. Damp chills seeped through his thin footwear, and as he emerged opposite St Frideswide's Church he was drawn by the warm glow cast by the torches that burned in the courtyard. For a moment he stood behind the canvas that hung between him and the stage, watching the shadows cast on it of those on the other side. He listened to the booming voices of the acting troupe and watched the distorted shapes moving across the canvas, sometimes small and insignificant, sometimes large and menacing. It seemed appropriate that they were enacting the Slaying of the Innocents.

As he watched, one shadow beckoned with what was clearly a sword. Cowering below this shape was the smaller form of a woman who pleaded for the life of her child with the voice of a man speaking in a higher pitch than he was used to. The sword fell and the shriek of the woman was accompanied by the more tentative cries of other youths imitating women. Falconer smiled, and listened to the soft-spoken man-woman telling Herod, who in shadow form now loomed across the canvas, that he had slain his own son. The Herod actor dashed his crown from his head and struck a pose to deliver his speech.

> *'Truly damned then I must be.*
> *My body rotten and my arms,*
> *Fiends from Hell do come in swarms,*
> *And I have caused so much woe*
> *To perdition I must go,*
> *My soul to be with Satanas.*
> *I die, I die, alas, alas.'*

As Falconer watched this shadow tableau, a horrendous shape entered from the right. It seemed taller than all those on the stage, though that might just have been the effect of the shadow and the angle of the lights that cast it. What was obvious were the impressive horns that contorted out of the creature's head. For a moment the figure seemed to fill the stage, then it staggered forward. Falconer was sure he saw another more human shape separate itself from the devilish form and retreat into the solid shadow at the side of the stage. It was a curious sequence of events that he could not fathom as part of a mystery cycle. Suddenly his puzzlement was broken into by screams and other shouts of alarm from beyond the canvas. Shadows fluttered hither and thither, but the figure of the Devil lay motionless on the floor with an elongated bar sticking up vertically from its back.

CHAPTER SIX

LUCIFER: Here will I sit now in his stead,
To exalt myself, not bend the knee;
Behold my body, my hands and head,
The might of God is marked in me.

The Fall of Lucifer

The reality that confronted Falconer as he came around the side of the backdrop that had screened him from the stage seemed tawdry in comparison to the shadow play. The figures on the stage were all smaller and the painted scenery was flat and lifeless. The two soldiers stood over the body with their wooden swords drooping in their hands. A woman with a bulky hairnet and linen cap bent over the prostrate form in the middle of the stage. As she moved to touch the instrument that jutted out of the dead man's back, Falconer called out, 'Don't touch it.'

When the woman looked up to see who had cried out, Falconer was startled by the face of a man peering out from under the head-dress. It was just another unreal image on top of all the other incongruities.

'But it's Stefano — he's been killed.'

The man dressed as a woman rocked back on his heels as Falconer knelt beside the figure of the Devil and gently eased the body on to its side. Unlacing the cords that held the all-enveloping mask in place, he pulled it off the dead actor's head. There was a gasp from both Herod and the kneeling actor as a monk's tonsure was revealed. Clearly they had been expecting the visage and flowing locks of Stefano de Askeles. This man's face was the soft, indoor face of a monk.

'What the hell's going on? I leave you all for a few minutes and everyone stops work.'

The sonorous tones of the man just presumed dead echoed across the courtyard. Falconer looked out to see a large and imposing figure emerging into the circle of light cast by the torches around the edge of the stage. He was dressed in similar long and flowing robes to the dead man, but under his arm he carried a gilded mask unlike the Devil's visage that Falconer had just removed from the body. His long blond hair was a reflection of the mask's golden image. He crossed the yard in three or four strides and stood at the edge of the stage, his face level with the crouching Falconer. He laid the gilded mask on the stage, where it sparkled in the torchlight. Its blank eyeholes surrounded by carved sun's rays seemed to look into everyone's soul — truly the face of God. The man's own eyes locked on to the regent master.

'And who are you, may I ask?'

Falconer ignored the question and bent over the body he still cradled in his arms to examine the murder weapon. Its shadow on the other side of the canvas had been distorted so that it had appeared to be nothing short of a spear. In reality it had a short wooden handle no longer than the span of a man's fist. The blade was embedded in the monk's back, but he could just make out the beginning of the metal part and it was curiously thick, unlike any knife he had ever seen. Before he satisfied his curiosity and pulled the weapon out, he noted the angle that it subtended with the dead monk's back. Definitely a blow struck upwards, not down from above.

By this time the leader of the troupe had realized what he was looking at was reality not artifice and had vaulted on to the stage. He stood over Falconer and the lifeless form of the Devil, whose other head, horns and all, lay to one side of the tableau, the white pools of its eyes staring to the skies.

'God in heaven. Who did this?'

Falconer took hold of the well-worn handle of the weapon, and pulled. It came out of the body with a sucking sound, and a trickle of bright red blood followed it.

'I don't know, but he killed using a carpenter's chisel.'

* * *

The King was punishing de Cantilupe for being associated with the guild-merchants and burghers whom Henry suspected of complicity with the robbers despoiling the countryside. The former Chancellor had returned to the King's hall in Beaumont as dusk fell. It was enough humiliation that he was obliged to run the gauntlet of cheap whores plying their trade virtually at the King's door. But when he reached the gateway into the main courtyard of the King's residence he had been abruptly halted by the janitor on the gate.

In the days of his former glory, he would have stridden straight through the gate, with the keeper grovelling on his knees. Now the man, a sturdy fellow with a red weather-beaten face, had the nerve to manhandle the ex-Chancellor. He placed his calloused hand on de Cantilupe's chest and forced him to stand outside the gate like a poor supplicant. The janitor had sent his boy in search of someone in authority who would decide whether the King could be disturbed at such a late hour. In the meantime, he placed a stool in the gateway and sat down on it, planting his feet firmly on the ground with his legs wide apart. With a beefy fist on each knee, he resembled an immovable tree stump, well rooted in the earth. De Cantilupe was left to pace angrily before him.

It was some considerable time before the boy returned, followed by a small stooping figure de Cantilupe didn't recognize. The skinny little man spoke briefly to the janitor in hushed tones, then approached the waiting ex-Chancellor.

'How can I help you?'

His voice was reedy, and the obsequiousness that de Cantilupe had expected was absent.

'Who are you?'

'I am the King's Usher of the Chamber,' the servant said in blustering tones of self-importance. De Cantilupe was shocked. In the hierarchy of the King's court this man was no more than Henry's dresser. He was being deliberately insulted. Still, he stayed his anger, for he knew it would do him no good — especially when his neck depended on his next few actions. He explained patiently to the lowly official that the King had asked him to discover who was colluding with the robbers that infested the countryside, and that he had urgent information. The little man abruptly turned and left him without so much as a bow to acknowledge his standing. Once again de Cantilupe was left with the impassive and tree-like janitor.

After a pause longer than the last, de Cantilupe saw a more familiar figure crossing the courtyard. He recognized the King's Marshal from his erect bearing — it was he who had ushered him into the King's presence that very morning. This time the man treated de Cantilupe as his former station demanded and apologized for the 'misunderstanding' that had kept him waiting. De Cantilupe understood that his penance had been served and gathered himself to provide the information the King wanted. He had spoken to several merchants in the town who were prepared to bear witness as a means of settling old scores. Some had been positively eager to do so. The Prior had assisted too with a name he spat out in distaste. As for himself, he knew whom he was going to sacrifice to the King if he was asked. Truth and justice were mere handmaidens at the court of expediency.

* * *

Bullock dealt expediently with the unhappy Prior of St Frideswide's, who could not understand why anyone should wish to kill Brother Adam. The monk was an inoffensive cleric who kept very much to himself. He diligently carried out all his duties without complaint. His involvement in the plays had been at the request of the Prior, so that he could check that the text was being adhered to. In reply to the Prior's unspoken question, Bullock reassured him that he did not think that was sufficient reason for his murder, and that the Prior should not blame himself for endangering the monk's life. Nevertheless, the churchman clearly felt responsible for the death, and hurried off to make arrangements for prayers to be said for the unfortunate Brother Adam. Bullock was left still wondering just why Brother Adam had been killed. He was relieved that Falconer was already present — it would save the embarrassment of asking for his assistance later. But before he could even raise the matter with him, Falconer's excited voice broke into his thoughts.

'I think I saw the murderer.'

Looking round, the constable was confronted by the regent master's piercing blue eyes. He had not been surprised to find William Falconer already in attendance when he arrived at the scene, alerted by one of the onlookers to the drama. The regent master seemed to have a knack of being around when a murder occurred. Bullock put it down to some sixth sense similar to that which he had seen on many a battlefield, where, as a foot soldier, he had come across many old soldiers whose very survival depended on that sense of knowing when the halberd's blow was aimed at them. He had seen death blows instinctively parried, when the soldier could not have seen what was coming with his eyes. He was sure Falconer sensed where the fatal blow was to fall almost before it happened. When he had spoken of his theory to the regent master, Falconer had laughed out loud, and poured scorn on the very idea. He preferred to think of his affinity with murder as a combination of coincidence and insatiable curiosity. However, he had never before been so close to a murder that he had actually seen the killer.

Hesitant, because he was one of only a few who knew that Falconer's eyesight was actually not of the best, Bullock enquired if he had recognized the man. Falconer frowned.

'Alas, he was just a shadow. And I don't know if what I saw was even real.'

The constable was puzzled by this statement — Falconer was usually so precise. He urged the regent master to explain.

'Everything happened on the other side of the backcloth on the stage. So what I saw was enacted in shadows cast on it by the torches in the courtyard.'

'That's a pity — but who did you think you saw?'

His friend closed his eyes, 'I will describe only what I actually saw, and draw inferences later when I have spoken to those who were on the other side of the canvas.'

Bullock knew Falconer's nature and accepted his desire to apply strict logic to everything that had happened that night.

'I saw the Devil enter from the right and somehow grow in size. For a moment he stood still, and then he lurched forward. At that moment it was as though his soul left his body, for I saw a human form detach itself from the Devil's shape and disappear.'

Bullock could not be more astonished at this fanciful description. Did Falconer really think he had seen the dying monk's departing soul? The regent master's eyes sparkled at the thought of having so intrigued his old friend. He was sure of what he had seen, and the way he described it was accurate. But he wanted to find out what the actors and any onlookers had witnessed before he confirmed his own suspicions.

The two friends crossed to the other side of the stage where the members of the troupe were huddled together, their fantastic robes pulled around them against the cold night air. An apparent argument was broken off as the two men approached, and their leader, de Askeles, looked flushed despite the cold. The others, three men and two women, looked guardedly at the constable, and at Falconer, who to them was an unknown quantity. Slightly apart from them stood a few men dressed as soldiers and Jews, and others dressed in ordinary clothes. One of this group was the man who had fetched the constable, and the rest Falconer therefore assumed were townsfolk, some of whom had been performing on the stage, and some merely onlookers who had remained around to watch the unfolding of a more exciting drama than they had originally expected. Otherwise, the stage was deserted, as the body had already been removed by the dead monk's colleagues. The torches were flickering in a last effort to ward off the darkness, and a doleful bell was chiming from the church tower. De Askeles broke the chilling silence.

'We're all tired and hungry and wish to get back to our inn. Can't you talk to us tomorrow?'

His remark was addressed to Peter Bullock, but it was Falconer who answered.

'This will not take long. I just wish to ask you a few questions while matters are fresh in your minds. You may have forgotten something vital by the morning.'

He did not add that the guilty one might also have had time to concoct a story by then. De Askeles was unsatisfied.

'Just who are you, anyway, to keep us here?'

'This is William Falconer. He is a renowned scholar and I value his insight into matters of suspicious death. He is known to the King.'

Falconer smiled behind his hand at the last statement. If he was at all known to the King, it was probably as a meddler in things that did not concern him. Still, the association served to impress those present, and de Askeles gave him room with a deep and rather mocking bow. Falconer asked Bullock to talk to the townspeople, both those who had been on stage as amateur actors and those looking on, then turned to the troupe of strolling players. He explained he would like to speak to each member of the troupe separately.

'And I will start with you, sir.'

He pointed at the man who was dressed as a woman, now holding his female locks in his hands, and led him across to the opposite side of the stage.

'Firstly, your name, please.'

'I am Simon Godrich, and I sing and act the women's roles in our plays.' He giggled nervously, and his fingers plucked at the false hair in the net.

'Please tell me what you saw tonight.'

'I am afraid I saw nothing until the Devil — the monk — fell at my feet. My role required that my eyes be downcast at that point. You see, my child has just been slaughtered, and it's to Herod that the Devil appears.'

'And who was playing Herod?'

'Robert. The one over there in the purple robe. Though why he should be given the part is beyond me. He's a better juggler than he is an actor.'

Falconer motioned to Godrich that he could go, then stopped him to ask another question.

'Before I took the Devil's mask off you said it was Stefano who had been killed. Why did you think that?'

'Because Stefano normally plays both the Devil and God — it feeds his conceit.'

'And you didn't know he had asked Brother Adam to assume the role tonight?'

Simon shook his head.

'Nor why he did or where he went?'

Falconer caught Simon's glance over to the huddle of actors awaiting their interrogation, and the scared look in his eyes. It might have helped Falconer if Godrich had revealed the true reason for his reluctance to say where de Askeles had been. But he was sure the man had been with Margaret Peper and wished to spare her shame. So he replied firmly, 'No, and no.'

'Thank you. Please ask Robert to come over.'

Falconer stood thinking as Godrich crossed the stage and spoke to the man dressed fancifully as a Saracen, with darkened features and a forked black beard. They seemed to exchange harsh words, and Herod looked long and hard at Simon Godrich, before casting an anxious glance at Falconer. He looked nervous as he walked slowly towards the regent master, as though reluctant to reach him. When he did, Falconer kept him unsettled by abruptly demanding his name.

'Robert. Robert Kemp,' came the faltering reply.

'And what did you see, Robert Kemp?'

'Nothing.'

Falconer was scornful. 'Nothing, when you were looking straight at the Devil? You were looking straight at him, weren't you? Your part certainly required it. Or perhaps you are not as good an actor as you like to think.'

'Of course I was looking at him. But the first I knew anything was amiss was when he pitched forward. Even then, for a moment I thought he had tripped on his robes. The Devil has long robes, you see, so that he appears larger than a man. That's why I saw nothing — he had his arms spread and raised above his shoulders. The robe must have masked anyone who might have been behind him.'

'Go on.'

'Well, when he fell, I realized he could not have tripped because it looked more as if someone had pushed him — hard — in the back.'

'And you saw no one.'

Kemp looked unsure of what he was about to say. 'I am not certain, but there might have been someone disappearing into the darkness off the stage.'

This was confirmation for Falconer that the shadow 'soul' he had seen did exist, and that it was more human than ethereal. It was only left for him to verify that Robert Kemp had also expected Stefano de Askeles to be underneath the Devil's mask, and he was satisfied that matters were beginning to fall into place. To his question concerning the whereabouts of de Askeles, he again got a nervous denial of any knowledge, though the man did offer something interesting about Margaret Peper and de Askeles. At that moment de Askeles himself stormed across the stage and demanded that they all be released.

'After all, what can the death of a monk have to do with us? We have only just arrived in Oxford.'

Falconer smiled. 'Oh, I don't think the monk was the intended victim.'

'And who was, then?' demanded de Askeles.

'You, of course.'

CHAPTER SEVEN

DOMINATIONS: Go to your places or run from hence
You have begun a perilous play
And shall soon know the consequence;
This dance will bring you a woeful way.

The Fall of Lucifer

William Falconer was faced with a dilemma. As ever, the curious death of the monk intrigued him, and he wished to exercise his deductive skills to solve the murder. However, there was also the pressing matter of Friar Bacon's mysterious alchemist. And although he did not have any teaching obligations so close to Christmas, he still had to exercise control over the impoverished students who were left in Aristotle's Hall for the winter celebrations. Although control was not exactly the word he would have chosen. It was the usual practice to elect a Lord of Misrule, so that the youngest and most unfortunate of his students had power over his seniors for a day in a topsy-turvy reversal of the accepted order. Indeed, it was common practice for the priories and abbeys in the vicinity to elect boy-bishops to the same end. They would be crowned with small mitres of cloth-of-gold, dressed in miniature versions of a bishop's cope, and bedecked in episcopal rings. Aristotle's Lord of Misrule would not be so adorned — Falconer did not have coin for such extravagance, and what he did have would be spent on good food and wine, something that his table rarely saw the year round. No, Aristotle's student lord would be lucky to get a paper crown (paper being as valuable to the regent master as gold was to the King), and Falconer's own wardrobe was too sparse to cut down a robe for the youth. He would, however, still be able to lord it for a day over those who dominated him for the rest of the year. Falconer hoped in this way that some of his students might learn a little humility. But his first concern was to resolve which mystery should have priority. The message from Bacon echoed round his skull again.

'No need to go as far as Germany to find this man.
Just seek his name from Omega to Alpha.'

Did not going as far as Germany mean going as far as France? If so, the alchemist might as well dwell in the Afric lands — Falconer could not afford to travel anywhere. But then surely the friar would have known that, and so the clue must mean look at home in England. Then it was not much of a clue, as Falconer had assumed the alchemist would be in Oxford anyway — or would have been when Bacon was in residence also. It was ten years since the friar had been sent to his solitary cell in France and deprived of all contact with the outside world. He could not know where the alchemist he sought was now, or whether he still resided in Oxford. The second sentence was even more confusing. Why were the first and last letters of the Greek alphabet back to front? Should he go back to the beginning to find the man? If so, what beginning? It was hopeless.

No, murder riddles were far easier to solve. Though, in the case of Brother Adam, Falconer was not entirely sure if he or de Askeles had been the intended victim, despite his confident assertion last night. He needed more information about de Askeles's whereabouts, and both the man himself and his fellow jongleurs were curiously reticent on that matter. The investigation would take some time, even though, ironically, he had actually been a witness to the murder himself.

What to do? Carry out his obligations to his friend Bacon, or assist his other friend Bullock? The decision was all but made for him when Peter Bullock burst into his private chamber. It was the morning following the murder, and the constable, always an early riser since his days as a foot soldier, expected to find Falconer also up and about. He was surprised to find the regent master still stretched out on his bed, a rough blanket pulled over his fully clothed body.

'You're not ill, are you?'

'What? Oh, no — I have a few things on my mind at present. I suppose I forgot to undress last night. And as it was so warm here and so cold outside, I decided to do my thinking this morning from the comfort of my bed.'

Bullock glanced around the room. 'I can see you have been preoccupied.' He was familiar with the impedimenta that normally surrounded Falconer, but usually it was arranged in some semblance of order. Now, everything was higgledy-piggledy. Some of Falconer's precious jars of herbs and aromatics lay on their sides, some unsealed, giving the room a cloying, heady scent. Books lay scattered across the table, most of them opened, the pages held down with whatever had come to the regent master's hand at the time. In some cases it was a rock, sheared off to reveal a strange pattern, in others a glass jar with something grey and unspeakable in it. In the centre of the table an animal skull, probably that of a deer, stared eyelessly at Bullock. Falconer saw Bullock's anxious gaze.

'Don't worry. I am not ill, nor am I mad. I am . . . was in the middle of trying to put down on paper some of the science I have learned over the years since Roger Bacon left us. I never thought to see him again and had resolved to record what I learned from him, and what I have deduced since. And as soon as I begin, he puts in an appearance.'

'He's back? Where is he, then?'

Bullock knew of Falconer's reverence for the strange, self-opinionated Franciscan, and didn't know he had returned to Oxford.

'Oh, he's not here in person. That would be too simple. No, he's sent a message which is as cryptic as his thoughts on the flying machine, and I am to work out this message and be his errand-boy.' He grimaced. 'I don't know if I have time even to solve the mystery of the Devil's death.'

A triumphant smile crossed Bullock's leathery face. 'That's fine. You see, I've solved it myself already.'

* * *

Margaret Peper was cleaning the Devil's robe, trying to wash off the blood that marred the back panel of the rich cloth before she stitched up the jagged tear. She was huddled down between the wheels of the wagon in an attempt to keep out of de Askeles's way, while he ranted and raved at all who had the misfortune to cross his path. The setback of the monk's death — for that was how he viewed it — was just another irritant in his preparations for the plays cycle. He was always annoyed by having to deal with amateurs, and now those very people were showing a marked reluctance to attend another rehearsal for fear of another tragedy. Even Margaret's own comrades in the troupe were a sullen bunch this morning, each suspicious of the other. Perhaps they were simply angry that the murderer had bungled it and failed to despatch the man who ruled their lives and browbeat them all. They all had cause to hate de Askeles — herself, John, Will because of the monkey, and even Agnes for his endless mocking remarks about her plainness.

She shivered as she recalled the piercing gaze of that regent master who had questioned them all the previous evening. His blue-eyed stare had seemed to penetrate to her very soul, and she had felt like confessing. He must surely know by now who was responsible. She busied herself with a swift and neat stitch, repairing the damage to the robe, and tried to put Falconer's eyes out of her mind. Above her she could hear someone moving around in the bed of the wagon, shifting heavy properties. She heard a crash followed by a curse — it was the voice of Stefano. He had obviously let something drop and hurt himself. Just as the noise of moving furniture began again, she felt the wagon sway as someone else climbed in at the rear. The muffled voices piqued her curiosity, especially when she heard de Askeles snarl some warning at the newcomer. She got to her feet and cautiously put her eye to an open seam in the canvas side of the wagon. Through the rent in the covering, she could just discern Stefano. But when the other person spoke she realized it was her husband, and he was frightened.

'I must tell them about it, or I will be accused anyway.'

'There is no need to tell them. They haven't the first idea who stabbed the monk, and they won't be able to work it out, because nobody saw anything. In a few days everyone will be too drunk to care, and it will all be forgotten.'

'But we were seen.'

'That I can resolve.'

De Askeles's voice was firm, but still Peper clutched at his sleeve and begged him. 'I am afraid. They will hang me.'

De Askeles snarled and wrenched his captive arm free of the other man's grasp. He thrust his angry face at Peper, the veins throbbing on his temples.

'Whatever you tell them will implicate you. So you'd better keep your mouth shut, for your own good.'

He swung round and stormed out of the wagon, leaping the gap from the tailboard on to the wooden staging where the play cycle would come to life. Margaret shrank back between the wheels of the wagon to avoid being seen. And above her John gave vent to his mixed fear and anger by pitching God's throne out of the back of the wagon and on to the stage, where it landed with a thump.

* * *

Edward Petysance was consumed with excitement. The man had vowed to him that he knew where the remains of the saint were and had promised to deliver them today. With a holy relic to rival that of St Frideswide, he could expect a lucrative income from pilgrims. And he could rub the superior Prior's face in the dirt when everyone abandoned his shrine for that of St Aldate. The troubadour had insisted that Petysance meet him in the church precisely at sext, and the priest now hurried impatiently from his nearby lodgings to St Aldate's. Entering through the church's south door, he was struck by the gloom in the main body of the nave. He cursed the lazy servitor who had obviously not lit the candles this morning. Hurrying up the aisle, he was aware of an imposing presence before the altar. He stopped and shielded his eyes from the light that filtered in through the stained-glass window above the altar. The man stood for a moment with the light turning his golden locks into a halo, then he strode down the steps to meet the priest. It was the troubadour, de Askeles.

'Father. I have good news.'

Petysance could not contain himself and clutched at the other's robe. 'You were able to obtain the saint's relics.'

De Askeles's face was solemn, his eyes pools of sorrow. 'Alas, I do not have the whole skeleton.'

The priest's face fell, his vision of a lucrative future shattered. But de Askeles smiled.

'But I do possess the saint's arm and hand. The very hand that blessed those who reverenced him while he lived. Come — I will show you.'

He put his arm over the priest's shoulders and led him towards the altar.

'Just think — more than seven hundred years since the sainted bishop's death and here lies his arm. You were lucky that we had travelled through Deorham earlier this year, and that the local prelate was prepared to part with such a rarity. Of course, if it were not for my ancestry . . .'

Petysance had heard a rumour that this jongleur was the bastard son of a cardinal, perhaps even of a pope. He certainly knew about St Eldad and the town where he had been killed. Even if the first were just rumour, the last was enough to convince him. He looked eagerly over the jongleur's shoulder. On the altar lay a long, narrow wooden box the length of a man's arm. The box was old and battered, and next to it stood a pewter pitcher and two goblets. A shaft of light from the window fell on the wood, and with trembling fingers Petysance lifted the lid. A dank, soily smell rose from the interior, but this did not deter the priest. There, on a bed of purple cloth, lay the arm-bones of a man, with the array of hand- and finger-bones wired to the end of the forearm so they splayed out as they had when covered in flesh. There was even a dull, gold ring with a green stone embedded in it on one of the fingers. The blessed hand of St Eldad. The priest's eyes sparkled with reverence and joy, and the jongleur smiled.

'I thought we might celebrate the occasion with a drink. Of course I only have water.'

De Askeles picked up the pewter jug and poured some water into the nearest goblet. The crystal clear liquid sparkled in the light. Then he handed the empty goblet to Petysance, and leaned over to fill it, passing the jug over the box on the altar. To the priest's amazement the liquid that poured forth had the ruby-red glow of a good Guienne wine.

'L-look,' he stammered, thrusting the goblet at de Askeles. As the troubadour tried to take it from his nerveless fingers, it fell between them, splashing a red stain over the grey stone surface of the altar. The sound of the goblet falling to the floor echoed through the gloomy church. De Askeles stood transfixed, staring first at the stain, then at the jug in his hand. He gently put the jug down, and stared at the shabby, grey bones lying in the box. He did not have to prompt the priest, who was also transfixed by the saintly bones.

'I have heard it said that Archbishop Sewal of York turned water into wine just before his death a few years ago. I would not have believed it could happen, if I had not just seen it with my own eyes.'

Just as de Askeles was about to reply, there came a strange ethereal sound from the depths of the church. An icy chill ran down Edward Petysance's back, and he hardly dared look up from the altar. De Askeles's eyes were already huge and rounded as he stared over the priest's shoulder. The reedy noise continued and Petysance slowly forced his gaze in that direction. The sound came from the gloom at the other end of the central aisle, where sat the heavy, bound chest holding the valuables of the church. As though from inside the chest, a slender figure arose and seemed to hover in the air. Though in darkness; the serene, pale face glowed with an inner beauty, and the priest had no doubt what the apparition was.

'The Virgin.'

He fell to his knees and clutched his hands together in prayer, his eyes tightly closed. Suddenly the strange noise stopped and Petysance opened his eyes again. The vision was gone. He staggered to his feet, and in a moment of doubt plunged down the aisle to where the figure had stood. Apart from the chest, there was nowhere a fully grown person could hide, and the chest was securely locked, with the only key at his waist. As de Askeles approached him, his whole body shook. The saint's arm was truly a powerful relic.

De Askeles cleared his throat nervously. 'About my payment . . .'

* * *

Bullock was now in full flight, waving the half-empty flagon of ale, with which Falconer had provided him, carelessly around the room as he explained his idea. Falconer nervously edged him away from the table where all his most precious books lay open. He dreaded the texts being smeared with splashes of ale. Oblivious of his friend's concerns, Peter Bullock made his case as clearly as he could — he knew Falconer would find the smallest loophole if it existed. He had spoken to all the townspeople present, from guildsmen who had volunteered to act in the plays to the onlookers who remained; indeed anyone he could find who had been in the yard at any point during the rehearsals.

'I even spoke to old Solomon, the Jew, who had been there before he went to work. Though why I bothered I know not. Someone more unlike his namesake you would be hard pressed to find. The poor unfortunate is no wiser than a new-born child.'

To Bullock it was clear nobody knew of a reason why anyone should seek to kill Brother Adam. Similarly, there was little evidence of a cause to do away with de Askeles, among the townsfolk at least. After all, he had only been in Oxford a few days.

'However, I do know of someone in his own troupe who hates him. I saw him outside the tavern where de Askeles and some of his band were entertaining the first night they arrived. He was full of anger and was spying on de Askeles. When the troubadours came out of the tavern, he hid himself and watched as de Askeles pawed at that pretty saltatore. I have since learned she is his wife. His name is John Peper, and he has motive enough to wish his leader dead. So, when you suggested de Askeles had been the intended victim, I started thinking.'

Falconer was unconvinced. 'Did you discover who the chisel belonged to?'

This brought a frown to Bullock's wrinkled face. He had not thought to find that out, and immediately regretted not doing so.

'Well, no. But the fact that the chisel belonged to someone does not mean he was the murderer. Perhaps he is just careless with his tools. Anyone could have stolen it — the site was very busy throughout the day, after all.'

'Have you determined where the rest of the troupe were when the murder occurred? The killer obviously could not have been Robert Kemp or Simon Godrich — they were on stage in full view of the audience at the crucial moment. And I would rule out de Askeles, as we believe he was the intended victim. That leaves Will Plome, John Peper, and the two women — Margaret Peper and Agnes Cheke.'

'You cannot think it was one of the women! Did you not say the shadow you saw wore breeches, not a long robe or skirt?'

'And how was the saltatore dressed when you saw her leaving the tavern?'

'Why — as a man . . .'

Bullock realized he had answered his own question, and blushed.

'This man has more enemies than Emperor Frederick himself! You'll be blaming it on the monkey next.'

Falconer pondered this most seriously. 'No. I could have been confused by the size of the shadow — small animal, large shadow — but it would not have had the strength to thrust the chisel in so deeply.'

Bullock snorted at Falconer's apparently serious consideration of the monkey's complicity. The regent master, however, continued along the track of his thoughts, mentally marking off each possible route.

'I regret now being so slipshod last night. I should have verified exactly where everyone was when I spoke to them. Even where de Askeles was returning from when he made his dramatic appearance. And I should still like to know whose chisel ended up in the Devil's back.'

The constable heaved a sigh and prepared himself for an interminable investigation.

Why did he always confide in Falconer when he knew the regent master turned a simple murder into a convoluted puzzle that took weeks to unravel? He supposed it was because Falconer always turned out to have the correct answer. He expected this case to be no different, so Falconer's next statement came as something of a surprise.

'But you must do what you think right. After all, you have uncovered a clue that I was unaware of through my negligence. If you say it's John Peper, then John Peper it is. I am far too busy to take it further myself, and I trust your judgement.'

Bullock could not believe his ears — Regent Master William Falconer was passing up the opportunity to investigate a murder. And one at which he had been present at that.

'Now, if you'll forgive me, I have a lot of work to do.'

He sat down behind his table and drew a large tome towards him. As he perused the tiny writing that filled its pages, he laid his hand on a sealed letter as though divining its contents. In a moment he seemed oblivious of Bullock's presence, and, when the astonished constable left, all that was visible was the top of his grizzled head of hair. But even as Bullock closed the door quietly behind him, Falconer's voice rang out.

'But don't forget to track down the carpenter.'

CHAPTER EIGHT

LUCIFER: I tell you all, do me reverence,
For I am full of heavenly grace.
If God comes back, I will not from thence,
But sit still here before his face.

The Fall of Lucifer

Thomas de Cantilupe was pleased with himself — his stratagem had worked. He rose late and did not bother to dress, merely tying the heavy robe he habitually wore in the bedchamber securely at his waist. He drew his favourite chair, which he was pleased to see de Cicestre had not dispensed with, close to the embers of the previous night's fire, and called for Halegod. The servant would no longer deal with him in the offhand manner he had used since the former Chancellor's unexpected arrival. De Cantilupe was once again in the King's favour, and his brittle confidence was restored. He settled back on the smooth oaken seat of the chair, worn down by the padded behinds of several chancellors, and gripped the arms in magisterial fashion: He reviewed the events of the previous day and smiled with satisfaction.

Returning through the hovels surrounding the King's residence in Beaumont, de Cantilupe had been growing in confidence. He led a motley group of merchants from Oxford, all of whom were prepared to swear that surprisingly highly placed officials and burghers were in collusion with the bands of robbers that infested the countryside around the town. The fact that all the names that were to be provided belonged to people who were business rivals of those in de Cantilupe's group or had offended them in some way in the past, was not something that mattered to Thomas. Nor would it matter to the King — Henry was used to having provided for him evidence of whatever misdeeds he fancied had occurred. Not that he was necessarily vain — in fact he was in many ways a modest and pious man. But a king can be sheltered from reality by the sycophants that surround him, whose continued existence depends on providing whatever 'truths' the king desires. De Cantilupe was a realist and a survivor, therefore more than familiar with this eternal fact. He would do what was necessary to ensure his own security. And salve his conscience with the thought that he was ensuring the release of the hostage burghers who had attended the King on that first day. Moreover, each of those who were being sacrificed must have committed some misdeed to be the object of the hatred of those he now accompanied.

In the presence of the King a long list of names was read out.

'Thomas Burewald, Edmund Inge, Walter Felde, Andrew Bodin . . .'

As the list progressed Henry's face grew more and more wrathful, as a sense of righteous anger imbued him. These were men whom he had trusted and given responsible positions with great rewards. He tugged at the two forks of his long grey beard and listened in stunned silence.

'. . . John Doket, Peter Stockwell, and the Jews Cresselin and Zerach.'

The recitation of the wrongdoers' names had ended, and Henry turned to de Cantilupe. 'Thank you, Thomas. I knew you could be trusted — this will not go unrewarded.'

De Cantilupe wriggled in his familiar chair and imagined what rewards he might extract from the King. A discreet cough brought him back to the present. Before him stood the stooped figure of Halegod, patiently awaiting his orders. It was uncanny how the man sensed the ex-Chancellor's new standing — the impatience with his presence that the servant had shown until this morning was gone. Now both understood their relative positions, and de Cantilupe was a generous master.

'I shall be part of the King's court for Christmastide. You may please yourself for the next few days.'

The old man allowed a faint smile to cross his normally sour features. Perhaps he could have the Christmas he had promised himself after all.

'Just ensure that the fires do not die in the hearths.'

* * *

Sweat poured from the brow of the alchemist as the heat in the room became almost insufferable. He had stoked the furnace until the centre of the flames seemed almost white, then placed the fire-clay crucible on the spout that projected from the top. The rush of heat at that point was almost too much to bear, and he could only position the crucible by holding it in a pair of long metal tongs. The chemicals began to melt as the heat transmitted itself through the wall of the fire-clay.

He scurried to the bench at the back of the room, where a clutter of glass flasks and metal mortars lay around the texts he now consulted. He was familiar with Aristotle's theory of the four elements — earth, water, fire and air — and the four properties of material bodies — hot and moist, cold and dry. It was obvious that cold water, which was wet, could be transmuted into hot air, which was still wet. The question was, could other bodies be transmuted into their primordial matter? He pushed aside the translation of Aristotle he had possessed for a number of years and drew towards himself the unbound sheaf of papers he had recently procured. His excitement when he had originally recognized their value was rekindled now as he scanned the information contained in them.

He had been visiting one of his colleagues when he saw the bundle of papers lying on the man's desk, bound with cord. From seeing just the first page, he had instantly realized what they were. Trying to contain his impatience, he had enquired whose property they were — the man in whose house he stood was a dullard who could barely understand Talmudic law. He learned that they had been left as a pledge by a master of the university in return for a few shillings. He had no difficulty in persuading his dull friend to pass the pledge on to him in return for a small profit. Hurrying home through the market, he had clutched the papers tightly for fear of losing such valuable alchemical texts.

Now he scanned the instructions again in order to continue his experiment. The secretive alchemist who had drafted the text had written everything in cryptic terms, but the terminology was familiar to the alchemist and he translated it as he read. White Queen was the term for sophic mercury, and Grey Wolf was antimony, a powerful purifier. He carefully measured out the required quantities from the array of jars that cluttered the shelves in front of him and turned back to the glowing furnace.

At first he tried to ignore the thunderous knocking at his street door, but when it continued, and was like to burst the door open, he cursed and decided he must respond to it. If anyone entered and discovered him at his present task, he could not vouch for the consequences. The valuable papers he quickly wrapped in their cloth and thrust behind a loose stone in the cellar wall. Crossing to the furnace, he reluctantly picked up his tongs to lift the crucible from the heat. Then he stopped — perhaps the interruption would not be long, and the chemicals would be ruined if he removed them now. Leaving them to blend, he rushed up the smooth stone steps from his laboratory. He slammed the cellar door behind him and turned the key in the massive lock. Dusting specks of chemical powder from his robes, he walked down the passage and opened the front door to be confronted by three burly men. Behind them, he could see an impromptu crowd of leering citizenry gathering, eager to see the discomfiture of another Jew. The man in the centre of the three spoke.

'Are you Zerach?'

Zerach — doctor, herbalist and secret alchemist — nodded in resignation, his shoulders slumped.

'I am arresting you in the name of the King.'

* * *

The message from Jehozadok had been urgent, and Falconer hurried down the back lanes south of the High Street, oblivious of the students and traders who flattened themselves against the cheap plaster walls of the houses as he passed. Turning down Jewry Lane, and thence into Fish Street, he paused momentarily before the two houses that served as the Jews' Scola and meeting place, which was also Jehozadok's home. Bursting anxiously through the door and up the stairs, he found the old man in his usual place, surrounded as always by books. Jehozadok's face was filled with alarm, but a smile of relief came as he peered at the new arrival.

'Ah, William, I knew it would be you. Everyone else treats me with a reverence I find irritating. As though I am elevated to holiness already, and they are just waiting for my body to leave this mortal world. Whereas you . . .' He motioned for Falconer to sit down. 'You treat me unceremoniously, as an old friend should. But you will want to know why I asked you to come. I have found your alchemist.'

Falconer leaned forward eagerly in the low chair, his knees almost on a level with his chest. The rabbi continued. 'Having told you to look close to home for the man Friar Bacon sought, I thought I had better do the same myself. Enquiring of my many visitors, I discovered this morning that one of our community has been purchasing many strange elements recently, including something referred to as Red King and White Queen.'

Falconer nodded — these were alchemists' names for sulphur and mercury. It sounded promising, and he listened carefully as Jehozadok spoke.

'I would have thought nothing of it, for this man is a doctor and uses all sorts of peculiar remedies. Many work, but some don't and I recall that some years ago he was in dispute with a student who sought a cure and was not satisfied. There was talk of necromancy even then. He draws attention to our people, and times are difficult enough for us already now the Caursins are offering moneylending services too. We depend for our existence on your Christian distaste for profiting from loans, coupled with your Christian need to borrow money. I remember when the Lateran Council's ruling that no Christian soul should speak to us or even sell us provisions was almost invoked here. There were a few anxious and starving weeks . . .'

The old man was rambling, and Falconer, anxious to trace Bacon's alchemist friend, gently broke into his reverie. 'How can you be sure it is the man I am seeking?'

Jehozadok returned to the present, and gazed triumphantly at Falconer with his half-blind eyes. 'Because he fits the clue you were given by the friar.'

'And the name of this man?'

'Ah, didn't I say? His name is Zerach de Alemmania, and he lives in Pennyfarthing Street.'

* * *

Despite his conviction that John Peper was the culprit, Peter Bullock was going through the motions of checking all other possible avenues. He doubted that William Falconer could keep away from the investigation for long — indeed he had been astonished that anything could have kept him away from it at all. Sooner or later, his friend would be asking questions and Bullock wanted to be certain he could answer them. He would show Falconer he could apply Aristotle's deductive logic himself, even if he had had no education at all.

As the watery winter sun struggled to rise above the yellowed town walls, and left dark shadows in the narrow lanes, he made his way towards the temporary stage in front of St Frideswide's Church, where the troubadours' wagon now also stood. He chose not to go to the inn where they were staying, guessing, rightly, that Stefano de Askeles would still be abed at this time of day. His aim was to speak to each of the troupe separately away from their master and compare their statements later.

Entering the silent yard below the steps of the church, he spotted a figure near the rear of the wagon and saw from the bald pate that it was the halfwit, Will Plome. He was dressed in the green and yellow parti-coloured jerkin of a Fool. His coxcomb cap with bells was tucked into the belt round his waist. He seemed to be talking to himself, and Bullock sighed at the appropriateness of his costume. It was only as he began to cross the yard that he heard a low cluttering in reply to Will's soft-spoken words. Suddenly the man capered away from the back of the wagon with something small, yet shaped like a human, bouncing on his shoulders. Bullock suddenly realized Plome had been talking to the monkey. Standing in the centre of the yard, he watched as monkey and man performed an impromptu dance, both clearly enjoying themselves. Will had a fur-trimmed robe in his hands and was whirling it around his head. Suddenly he drew a long thin object from his belt and repeatedly thrust it into the folds of the gown. He gibbered with delight as he let the gown fall to the ground, and the monkey's voice redoubled the rejoicing. Then Will became aware of the observer and stopped his capering abruptly. His brilliant smile fell away, and he clutched the wriggling monkey to his breast. He dropped his weapon, and stood stock still as Bullock approached him, his eyes downcast like someone caught stealing.

Bullock smiled at him and tried to reassure the man that he meant him no harm. In his mind he wrestled with the thought that Will might have been re-enacting Brother Adam's murder. But had he taken the central role? Still, he had to come round to asking the obvious question some time. Might as well get it over with straight away.

'Will Plome, can you tell me where you were when the monk was killed yesterday?'

The shaven-headed Fool shook his head.

'Nowhere.'

'Come now, you must have been somewhere. God is everywhere, but we mere mortals have always to be somewhere.'

The monkey clambered around Plome's shoulders, its long tail working like a third arm. Bullock noticed with fascination that its privy parts were red and blue. Finally it squatted with its arms around Plome's bald head, its chin resting on the hairless dome. To Bullock it resembled some bizarre living piece of headgear. Two pairs of eyes stared at the constable, the lower ones limpid and full of pleading.

'I . . . I was on that side of the stage, where the Devil comes out. But I didn't see anything.'

'How can I believe that? The murderer must have passed you to get on stage, and off again. You don't expect me to accept that he could do that without your seeing him, do you? Perhaps you were the murderer.'

Will Plome's wail was echoed by the monkey, who leaped from his shoulders, scuttled across the yard, and disappeared into the back of the wagon. The Fool would have followed him, but Bullock grabbed his arm.

'You didn't kill him, did you?'

'I wanted to,' screamed the frightened man, his face red all the way to his bald crown. 'He hurt Ham.'

'Ham? Who's Ham?'

'My monkey.' He pointed at the wagon. 'He swung Ham by his tail and hurt him. So I wanted to hurt him in return. He should have died.'

Plome wrenched his arm from the constable's grasp, and with a gait that resembled Ham's followed the monkey into the wagon. His head popped back out almost immediately, and he called to the stunned Bullock, 'Don't tell Stefano I was here. He says I shouldn't take Ham out of his cage. Says he's too valuable to lose.'

As the constable paused to pick up the weapon Will had dropped, which turned out to be no more than a twig, a female voice hailed him.

'What have you done to poor Will?'

He turned, to be confronted with the sour-faced woman Agnes Cheke. She stood hands on hips, her stocky, peasant frame seeming to grow out of the packed earth on which she stood.

'And why should I have done anything to "poor Will"?'

'I heard him scream — and you upset the monkey. I heard that too.'

Bullock warmed to this ugly woman, who stood up for those she deemed incapable of defending themselves. In other circumstances he might have sought to bed her. He liked strong women and did not care about their looks — he was no manuscript illustration himself, with his crook back and leathery, wrinkled face. But he was here on official business, and this was the opportunity to question Agnes about her movements yesterday. Perhaps he would get on to the other matter afterwards.

'He'll be all right. It's you I want to talk to.'

'Oh? And what about?'

'Tell me where you were yesterday when someone was pushing a chisel into the heart of that unfortunate monk.'

* * *

Falconer hastily took his leave of Jehozadok, and left the serenity of the Scola to enter the bustle of Fish Street again. Fletchers' and cutlers' shops occupied the ground floor fronts of the houses that lined the east side of the street, though many of the houses actually belonged to Jewish families. The street itself should have afforded easy passage to a cart, but at this time of the day the route along it was made perilous by the innumerable ramshackle stalls of the fishmongers and greengrocers that lined each side. Down the centre of the street ran the stinking channel that took human ordure and the rubbish of the market down to the river. A similar stew of humanity occupied the west side of the street, but on that side most of the shops were vintners.

Negotiating the hurly-burly, Falconer entered the narrow lane in which Zerach de Alemmania's house stood cheek by jowl with Bull Hall, where students of Civil Law resided. Passing the entrance to the hall, Falconer stopped at the next building, a substantial stone house on two floors with a solid oak door. He immediately realized there was something dreadfully wrong — the door was open wide to the street. No Jew in England, living in day-to-day fear of the community surrounding him, would leave his door open like that. Cautiously, Falconer put his head inside the dark passage and called Zerach's name. There was no reply.

Stepping over the threshold, he trod on a hard, angular shape hidden in the shadow cast by the half-open door. Bending down to pick it up, he realized it was a large and well-worn key, its surface pitted and scratched. He wondered if something had happened to Zerach as he sought to lock the street door, but when he tried the key in the lock it did not turn. He pushed open one of the doors leading off the passage, and peered into a large, dark room. The shutters were tightly closed across the only window, giving out on to Pennyfarthing Street, and the only light was from a single rushlight. By the feeble flickering flame, Falconer could see a stack of books sitting on the end of a large table that dominated the centre of the room. Scattered across the surface of the table were other books and papers. He crossed the room and leafed through the chaos that spread out from the chair set at the table. To one side lay the *Abecedarti Danielis Prophete* — the Book of Dreams — and to the other were several texts of Aristotle which were quite familiar to him. In the centre, and clearly the text that had occupied Zerach's mind most recently, were several sheets of paper with spidery writing all over them. Falconer had only to glance at one to realize they were part of the *Secretum Secretorum* of Aristotle, a copy of which Roger Bacon had given him. Knowing how his friend cherished the rare document, its presence in Zerach's house only served to confirm that the Jew must be the alchemist he sought. Now all he needed to do was to find the man. Perhaps if he found the lock the key fitted, he might discover some clue to his disappearance.

Returning to the main passage, he spotted another door at the far end. Despite being an internal door it had a heavy metal lock, and Falconer felt sure this must be the partner to the key he held in his hand. It fitted perfectly and turned smoothly. Pushing the door open, he was met by a blast of heat and was aware of a red glow at the bottom of the steps that descended from where he stood. He briefly recalled a time he had descended into another cellar, when an accidental ingestion of a drug had convinced him he was entering hell. This time he was in full control of his senses, but still he went down the steps with care, in case some human agent reacted unpleasantly to his presence.

There was no one in the low-ceilinged room, and the source of the heat and infernal glow proved to be a clay furnace that still burned hot despite being unattended. On top of the funnel above the fire, a clay dish was filled with the ashy remains of some chemical. Whatever experiment was being conducted here had failed because the experimenter had been interrupted and unable to return to his work. Falconer crossed to the bench that stood against one wall, above which was a remarkable collection of vials, jars and pitchers. Each one was carefully labelled, the contents named in a bold and clear hand. Falconer scanned the labels: mercury . . . vitriol . . . sal ammoniac . . . saltpetre.

It was truly an alchemist's collection of materials, but where was Zerach? Someone meticulous enough to label all the jars, and to lock the cellar door behind him, surely would not have voluntarily left an experiment half done. Finding a pitcher of water on the floor beside the furnace, he doused the glowing coals to prevent a fire. They spat and crackled like a horde of demons from hell, but then sank back into a blackened mass that could only steam impotently.

Falconer carefully locked the secrets of the cellar away and hid the key inside the Book of Dreams on Zerach's table. He stepped outside the house, shutting the door firmly behind him, and wondered what he should do next about delivering Roger Bacon's letter.

* * *

Solomon dropped the bolt on the little hut that he used as his sentry-box each night and wedged it fast with a heavy stone. The stone was a corner from a larger monument and had ancient letters carved on it. But they meant nothing to Solomon — the satisfying weight of the stone was what he needed. Happy that his meagre possessions were safe in the hut, he pulled his rags around him and set off towards East Gate. It did not occur to him that the hovel was made of weak daub, and if anyone wanted to steal his possessions they could push their way through the side wall of the hut more easily than breaking down the door. Nor did it cross his mind that no one would want to steal his possessions anyway, consisting as they did of a cheap mutton-fat lamp and a blanket as tattered as his clothes. All he knew was that in this world you could not trust the Christians, and there were Christians all around.

The roadway leading into East Gate was churned and muddy, for the sun was high enough to have melted the nightly frost. Oblivious to the filth that squelched up through his cracked and worn-out footwear, Solomon plodded along at the roadside thinking only of his bed in his sister's house. Saphira had looked after him from the days of his sickly childhood. It had not made her marriage a very happy one, as her big brute of a husband Covele had resented the attention she paid her brother. Solomon had secretly rejoiced when he died, and his sister had not remarried. He and Saphira were getting on in years now and rubbed along together in a set routine. And that was what he liked — unusual occurrences frightened him.

That was why the events of the other night kept turning over in his mind. Oh, he saw lots of things from his vantage point overlooking the road out of East Gate, where he spent every night. It was surprising how many people conducted secret assignations on that road when they should be securely locked up inside the city. He had seen friars of all orders meeting women. And recently he had seen someone from the city meeting a ferocious-looking wild man, who must have been from one of those robber bands Saphira said plagued the countryside. He'd seen the same townsman the other day working on the stage for the play-actors, and discovered his name was Ralph. Not that he would be telling anyone what he saw — Jews kept their mouths shut in England if they knew what was good for them. Or so his father had said when he was small. He still wondered what had happened to his father, who had disappeared just before the family moved from their home in Lincoln and came to Oxford.

Once through East Gate it was his habit to turn left down the narrow alley that ran immediately inside the walls — too many people made fun of him if he went down the main street. On this occasion someone behind him turned into the alley too, and he quickened his pace instinctively, thoughts of robbers still on his mind.

But neither could he shake off the vivid memory of the scene that had presented itself the other night. Hearing an unfamiliar sound, he had looked out of his sentry-box and seen, only a few paces away, someone digging in the ground. The door to his hut squeaked as he swung it further open and the figure lifted its face towards him. The shock of recognition had stunned him. He was churning the moment over in his mind again and failed to hear the slap of running feet behind him. It was only when an excruciating pain lanced through his head that he half turned to see the pale, contorted features that loomed over him. His pursuer raised his weapon again and brought it down once more on Solomon's already shattered head. The Jew fell in a heap in the darkest corner of the alley, his open, unseeing eyes staring at the weapon his assailant had dropped to the ground. It was the curiously carved stone that should have been securing his hut.

CHAPTER NINE

GOD: Say, what array do I find here?
Who is your prince and principal?
I made thee, O Angel Lucifer,
And here thou wouldst be lord over all!

The Fall of Lucifer

For Peter Bullock the day was not progressing well. His examination of Agnes Cheke had revealed that she had been on her own when the murder occurred, cleaning some of the costumes, so no one could vouch for her not being the killer. It also uncovered in her another person who hated de Askeles. She had been quite frank about it to the constable, her plain face set like stone.

'Did I kill the monk? That's for you to find out. Did I wish Stefano dead? Of course. He just does not give up, you see. Using and abusing people.'

'And you?'

'Well, I know I am not the prettiest woman on this earth. But I do not need reminding of it day in and day out.'

'Then why do you stay with the troupe?'

The woman's plain face creased in a sad smile. Why, because she had never earned so much as she did now. She had done so many jobs in her life she could not remember them all. Seamstress, cook, housekeeper, she had tried them all. She had been a very plain girl, who had grown into an even plainer woman. That of itself was no problem for her — she knew she had all the skills required of a good wife. The trouble had been finding a good husband. The man she had married, a miller by trade, had expected her to tolerate his violent moods simply because she was not fair of face.

'If you leave me, who will have you?'

That was his regular taunt, for he little knew that she did not care if anyone else would have her. One day, drunk, he made to hit her and she swung the iron pot she held at his head. The blow connected and he fell like a sack. Not caring if he was alive or dead, she took him at his word, and left with only a bundle of clothes. She had never felt so happy as she did that day. With nothing to sustain her other than her own resources, she soon discovered hard work was not difficult to find. And a washer of clothes, a cook or a seamstress she might have stayed, until one day she jestingly used the little knowledge of palmistry she had learned from her grandmother on the hand of a woman she worked with. Soon other women were coming to her to have their futures explained. She immediately gave up her exhausting labour and made her living by using her growing skills in palmistry to tell people what they wanted to hear — or what she thought they ought to hear. De Askeles had come across her at a country fair near Canterbury and recruited her for his growing band of troubadours, which was already gaining itself a reputation — though sometimes she wondered if her skills as a seamstress had attracted him more than her palmistry. But yes, money was why she tolerated de Askeles.

'Stefano is good at finding the full and open purse. And anyway, Will needs me to protect him. Without me, he would do something silly.'

'Silly? What do you mean — can't he control his temper?'

Agnes realized she had said too much. 'Did you know I read palms? Shall I read yours?' She took one of Bullock's calloused fists in her hands, and gently opened the fingers.

'The left hand is best because it is less marked with cuts and creases from great use. See this line here?' She drew a finger across his palm to the calloused pad on its edge. 'That is your line of life — but don't be fearful. It is a long one.'

Bullock snorted. 'That's not too difficult to tell. Some would say I was well advanced in years already.'

Agnes ignored him, and continued tracing the lines on his palm with her finger. She frowned and spoke in a serious tone. 'I must tell you that the midward line here . . .' she pointed at a crease that ended between his third and fourth fingers '. . . betokens death from a sword wound.'

'Thank God for that. At least I shall not die in my bed in piping old age, rendered blind and deaf.' Bullock guffawed, and tried to pull his hand from Agnes's grasp. Before he could do so, she held his little finger and peered at the creases on it.

'This tells you how many wives you will have.'

'That I certainly do not wish to know.' He clenched his fist, and turned from Agnes in embarrassment. 'Where might I find Margaret Peper?'

'With her husband. Where else? Now I must go and make the wagon ready for use as our dressing room.'

Agnes's face was hard and impenetrable. She abruptly walked away from the constable and went to the wagon into which Will Plome had disappeared. It was a moment before Bullock realized that she had avoided explaining her statement about the halfwit. He sighed and decided he would have to ask again at a later date, if it became necessary. He did not want to risk annoying Agnes — he thought that might be like holding a sword aloft in a lightning storm. In any event, he was still convinced that John Peper was his prey, and a talk with Margaret Peper could settle the matter once and for all.

* * *

Petysance had quickly fashioned a much more opulent box for the arm of St Eldad than the battered one de Askeles had transported it in. The arm now lay on padded velvet inside an ash casket that was bound in brass at the corners. Perhaps when the revenue from pilgrims started rolling in he could bind the box in silver like the one which held the bones of St Frideswide. No — if hers were encased in silver, then the arm must be bound in gold. But that was for the future. Now, he could not wait a moment longer, and he proceeded to spread the news of his holy relic by the most reliable method possible. He told John Cope, the old fishmonger whose stall was hard by the walls of St Aldate's Church, that he now possessed a holy relic which had already proved its powers by turning water into wine. He did not reveal the apparition of the Virgin, saving that for later. He need not have bothered, for the miracles multiplied anyway as the story was spread. Every person who bought from the fishmonger's stall was told about the miraculous arm of St Eldad, and every purchaser of fish told the next person he met in his travels, be he stallholder or neighbour. Suddenly the market was buzzing with talk about how the relic had converted water into wine, made the blind to see, and finally raised the dead. It was surely destined to be a greater curer of the sick than even St Frideswide's remains.

Crowds began to gather at the door of the church, jostling each other to be at the front when the relic was produced. But Edward Petysance had no intention of wasting the drama of the occasion by simply lifting the bones in front of such an impromptu rabble. He slipped out through the church door and closed it firmly behind him. For a while the crowd grew noisier, demanding to see the holy arm, until at last he raised his hands above his head. Gradually silence descended, and he explained what he planned to do.

'I shall carry the relic of St Eldad at the head of the procession which will precede the start of the play cycle in two days' time. Then and only then will you be able to see its miraculous powers.'

The crowd roared its approval, and so missed Petysance's quiet comment of satisfaction to himself.

'And it will all be played out right on St Frideswide's doorstep.'

As the excited crowd dispersed and the priest returned to gloat over his prize, Stefano de Askeles ambled through the market on his way to the temporary stage in front of the priory church. Beside him was Margaret Peper, dressed now in the modest robes of her sex, which still did not fully conceal the lithesome nature of her step. Behind the two walked a sullen John Peper, staring at de Askeles's broad back and clearly wishing that the chisel had been embedded in it last night, and not in error in the monk. De Askeles laughed as he heard the chatter around him about the appearance of St Eldad's arm. He cast a knowing glance over his shoulder at Peper.

'It reminds me of the time the Archbishop brought the bones of St Martin to Abingdon. They had already been working miracles up and down the country. A cripple got to hear of it and told his friend the blind man that the miraculous bones were arriving. The cripple climbed on his friend's shoulders and urged him away.

'"Why are we going this way?" said the blind man. "Isn't the Archbishop coming in the other direction?"

'"Exactly," said the cripple. "We earn far too much money from begging to risk being cured. Let's get away as fast as we can!"'

De Askeles roared with laughter, and Margaret's gentler peals joined in. John Peper was clearly not amused, and when de Askeles put his hand intimately on the back of Margaret's neck he stormed off into the crowd. Margaret sighed and made to follow him, but de Askeles grabbed her arm.

'Leave him. He'll cool down — we've got more rehearsing to do. It looks as if I'll have to be God and the Devil both after all.'

* * *

Peter Bullock's suspicions about John Peper's reason for wishing to kill de Askeles were confirmed when he saw the imposing leader of the troupe enter the courtyard with Margaret Peper on his arm. They were halfway across the open yard before de Askeles saw the constable. He stopped momentarily, then painted a smile upon his face, and hailed Bullock. 'Ah, the guardian of the law has returned. But without his nosy friend, I see. Do you want to speak to me?'

'Actually no, it's Margaret Peper I really came to see.'

The woman looked as though she wished she could disappear, but de Askeles thrust her forward.

'Very well. I have to start rehearsing the plays again anyway.' With that, he strode off towards the front of the stage, where a knot of townsfolk and monks were gathered, nervously awaiting their instructions for the day. De Askeles called out to them as he approached. 'Don't worry, no more murders are envisaged for today. So you can concentrate on getting your words right.'

Bullock left him to it and guided Margaret to a quiet corner of the yard. Before he could begin to ask her anything, words poured from her.

'I didn't see anything, you know. I wasn't anywhere near the stage when it happened. And before you ask, no, I wasn't with Stefano either.'

'Was I going to ask that?' queried Bullock, certain that at some point he would have. At least it confirmed his suspicions about a liaison and saved him the awkwardness of broaching the matter. Still, he wondered if he could entirely take her at her word. 'You must think there is good reason for my asking it.'

Her face clouded. 'Why does everyone assume that I enjoy the attention he pays me? I don't, you know.'

'Your husband clearly thinks you do,' remarked Bullock.

'John just doesn't understand that we'd both be beggars on the street if I didn't keep Stefano happy. He only keeps John on because of me — John's not the best actor in the kingdom, after all.'

Bullock continued his blunt line of questioning, though it had not exactly had good results with the others. He was beginning to realize how difficult it was to emulate William Falconer.

'So what were you doing when the murder took place?'

'I'd just watched John play his part — he liked me to do that.'

'What part was it?'

'Noah.'

Bullock paused, then said, 'Go on.'

'Then I went down the lane a little to get away from the hangers-on. I need to keep supple, so I do exercises every night and didn't want some idiot gawking at me.'

The constable drove the image of Margaret somersaulting down Fish Street from his mind and asked her to continue.

'That's it. I came straight back when I heard the commotion start, and the rest you know.'

Bullock felt frustrated. Why was it none of the troupe could vouch for the whereabouts of any other? Apart from those on the stage, every one of them seemed to have been on their own. He only had John Peper left to question. Then a thought occurred to him. 'You say John was playing the part of Noah?'

Margaret nodded.

'I've seen that play performed before. Do you follow the usual practice and build the ark on stage?'

'Yes, Stefano insists that we do it properly — it's quite a spectacle.'

'So Noah would be carrying carpenter's tools? Including chisels?'

Margaret didn't reply, but Bullock already knew the answer from the look in her eyes.

* * *

In Aristotle's Hall the handful of students who would remain in residence for the Christmas festivities were emptying their purses of all the coins they could find. It was a small, sad pile that sat on the long, battered table in the communal hall. Thomas Symon, the most senior clerk present, counted the coins again. But however many times he did so, it did not amount to enough. For several weeks Thomas and the others had been following the growth of the bristly red sow that their neighbour was fattening in the yard next to the students' hall. They had looked on with pleasure as the pig's cheeks filled out and its tiny eyes sank into the fleshy face. The students were not interested in the rotund body of the pig, but when it was slaughtered they had agreed to purchase the head. Boiled, it would provide a magnificent feast to mark Christmastide. Now it seemed they did not even have enough to buy the head.

One student, a scrawny youth with a pock-marked face, suggested they could work in the fields to earn a few marks. Thomas, a farmer's son, snorted his derision.

'Stephen. There is no work on a farm at this time of year. Most animals have been slaughtered already, and if you think anything grows at this time of year you're a bigger fool than I took you for.'

The scrawny youth scowled. What did he know of the countryside? His father was a silversmith to the King and lived in Westminster. The nearest cows had been a good mile away from where he lived. Thomas's rebuke prompted him to offer another suggestion.

'Then we should take our weapons and go and rob some rich traveller coming through Bagley Wood.'

'If you think that, then you're a fool for certain.'

The regent master's sharp tones cut across the students' chatter. Falconer was sitting hunched over the fire in the hearth at one end of the hall, and his charges had all but forgotten he was there. Deep in thought, he had been almost ignoring their conversation until he heard Stephen foolishly suggest robbery. He turned from the warmth of the flames and glared at the youths seated round the scratched and battered table.

'The King has just arrested twenty townsfolk for merely being suspected of involvement with a robber band. They are to be hanged after Christmas. So don't suggest robbery even in jest.'

The youths were shocked into silence — they had not heard their master speak so harshly before — and sat staring at the forlorn heap of coins on the table. Falconer regretted his outburst, but thought it best not to soften his words — Stephen Cosyn was stupid and impetuous enough to carry out his ill-conceived ideas if not firmly stopped. He returned to tossing plans around in his own head. He had to find a way to save at least Zerach de Alemmania from the noose, if not the other townspeople. He had been surprised to hear from another master of the unscientific way that the supposedly guilty men had been identified. It offended all his tenets of good deduction, based on Aristotelian logic. Successful solution of crime depended on careful comparison of known truths, from which a greater truth could be inferred. Hadn't he used this method himself to solve several murders in Oxford? That the King could be so easily beguiled into believing the words of known rivals of the supposed malefactors annoyed Falconer, particularly as a former Chancellor of the university had been instrumental in collecting the so-called 'facts'.

His informant had referred to de Cantilupe's role in providing the King with the culprits, and it had been the first Falconer knew of the ex-Chancellor's presence in Oxford. In his time at the university, the man had been a worthy adversary of Falconer's, challenging the regent master's role in murder investigations. Curiously, Falconer respected him for his clear thinking, which made it all the more irksome that he should be involved in Zerach's arrest. He had thought of approaching de Cantilupe to help him convince the King of the citizens' innocence, but knew it was useless. De Cantilupe was obviously prepared to sacrifice them for his own ends, and was unlikely to change his mind for the sake of a regent master who had been a thorn in his side in the past.

'Master.'

Falconer became aware of Thomas Symon standing over him. An anxious look on his face betrayed the fact that he was nervous about disturbing Falconer's thoughts. The master forced a smile to his lips.

'What is it, Thomas?'

'If we are not to have our feast, we thought at least we could celebrate in style.'

'And?'

'We wondered if we could elect a Lord of Misrule for Christmastide.'

Despite his thoughts on this subject only recently, Falconer frowned at the idea of allowing the custom in his hall just now. He was not in the mood to allow one of his unruly students to govern the hall during the Christmas period. If Stephen Cosyn were elected, he might decree all sorts of silly actions, and Falconer and the other students would be bound by custom to observe his commands. Even bishops and kings bowed to the ancient custom and did what the poorest, most menial person elected as Lord of Misrule or boy-bishop demanded of them. He smiled to soften the refusal. Then he was suddenly animated as though struck by lightning. That was the answer, of course. Why had he not seen it before? Falconer leapt from his chair, almost throwing Thomas on his backside. His previously forced smile spread into a huge natural grin.

'Thank you, Thomas. You have solved a very difficult problem.'

Thomas was bewildered. 'I have?'

'Yes, indeed. Now come with me. You and I are going to see Master de Cantilupe. And the rest of you — elect your Lord of Misrule. Even if it has to be Stephen Cosyn.' The other students groaned. 'Oh, and go and pay for that pig's head now, before anyone else buys it.'

To everyone's astonishment, the normally penurious master drew several coins from his purse and scattered them across the table. The next moment he was out of the hall with Thomas Symon in tow.

'Oh, Lord, all honoured shalt Thou be,
The earth it dries . . . before me,
But till Thou command me
From here I will not fly.
When all the water's gone away,
Sacrifice shall I this day . . .'

The words dried on John Peper's lips. De Askeles, dressed as God in gilded robes but without his mask, strode angrily across the stage.

'No, no, no.' He recited Peper's lines perfectly himself.

'When all the water's gone away,
So shall I as soon as may,
Sacrifice to you this day.

'How many times have we done this play? And still you cannot recall the words.'

John Peper, dressed as Noah in a long blue robe, stammered in anger and fear at Stefano's overbearing manner.

'I . . . I know the words. It's just the last few days . . .'

He left the end of his excuse unsaid and rushed off the stage. De Askeles glared at his retreating back, and pointedly recited God's words at the end of the Noah play.

'My blessing to you I give here,

For vengeance no more shall appear.

So fare thee well, my darling dear.'

The words stung Peper, who stripped off the blue robe at the edge of the stage and stormed down the flight of creaky steps that led to the beaten earth of the courtyard below. In a blind rage, he ran straight into the solid figure of Oxford's constable.

'Ah, the very man I was seeking,' murmured Peter Bullock, clutching Peper's arm in his calloused grip. At first the troubadour wriggled to free himself, but then he realized it was pointless. The constable's grip was too strong, and he could not keep avoiding him. When Peper relaxed, Bullock let him go and he subsided into a heap on the seat that stood beside him. It was God's throne on the stage but viewed close to, the gilding was inexpert and the moulding flat — a painted simulacrum. The overall effect was cheap and tawdry. A tired smile flickered across Peper's lips, as unreal as the throne he sat upon.

'And what is it you want to know?'

'Where you were when the monk was killed.'

Peper had known this was the question he would be asked, but still he had no answer. At least, not one that he could give the constable. There was a glimmer of fear in his eyes, and he cast a glance at de Askeles, who still strutted on the stage, reciting the whole of God's speech to Noah.

'I cannot recall.'

'Come now, it was only the other night. Let me remind you. You had just completed the scene you were enacting just now. You came off stage. Where did you go?'

Once again that glance at de Askeles, who now was haranguing one of the amateur performers.

'I cannot say.'

'Then perhaps you can tell me what you did with the bag of carpenter's tools you had then, and where they are now.'

Peper hung his head in silence, not sure what he could say. Bullock grimaced and drew himself up as he used to do on parade.

'Then, if you cannot tell me where you were, I have no choice but to arrest you for the murder of Brother Adam.'

CHAPTER TEN

GOD: Amongst all the angels there was none, as you know,
That sat so closely to my Majesty.
I charge you fall till I say 'No'
In the pit of Hell evermore to be.

The Fall of Lucifer

With only a few days to the start of the Christmas celebrations and the presentation of the plays cycle by Stefano de Askeles's troupe, Oxford was filling with peasants from the surrounding countryside. At this time of year they actually had some time to spare from the normal agrarian grind, and the possibility that another murder might be played out before their eyes added an extra spice to coming to see the plays. It was some disappointment therefore when the milling crowds discovered that the town constable had arrested the murderer. But there was still the hope that the new holy relic of St Eldad might produce a miracle, and the general excitement was increased by the numerous side-shows that now filled the narrow streets of the town.

Edward Petysance felt a new confidence in his ability to draw the crowds to his church and strolled around observing the mummers and acrobats sweating to earn their money despite the chill that hung in the afternoon air. Fish Street was the most popular spot to perform as it ran from north to south, and the low sun shone down its length casting giant shadows. Near the South Gate, a crowd garnered round the shambling figure of a performing bear, then reeled back in a body when the trainer holding its lead caused it to lunge at those standing closest. Everyone gasped, then giggled nervously to reassert their bravado. Truth to tell the bear was old, and its fur hung lank and dull from its shrunken haunches. But when it reared up on its back legs and blew its noxious breath through yellowed teeth at master and peasant alike, it seemed a fearsome creature.

Further along there were several bastaxi — puppeteers — retelling familiar stories through the mannequins they manipulated. Some were crude, stiff figures carved as soldiers and fixed to the ends of rods that the puppeteers pushed together from opposite ends of a table set up in the street. The swords at the ends of the outstretched arms rattled together as the bastaxi retold stories of Crusader victories. They attracted the uneducated and gullible, but Petysance far preferred the animated puppets that enacted domestic scenes on top of an upright cloth booth that hid the puppeteer from sight. There was one close to St Aldate's Church and he lingered at the back of the crowd to watch. The booth was the height of a man and had a tiny stage atop it like the full-size stage in front of St Frideswide's. Magical figures manipulated from below by the hidden puppeteer played out a quarrel between a lascivious wife and a cuckolded husband. The audience before the booth roared with laughter at some reference to the husband's lack of prowess, just as a voice behind Petysance spoke into his ear. He turned to be confronted by the Prior of St Frideswide.

'I beg your pardon — what did you say?'

The Prior's face looked as though he had swallowed vinegar thinking it to be wine.

'I was reminding you of the Dean of Salisbury's observation on histriones.' The Prior used the rather derogatory term for actors. 'There are three types — those who transform their bodies with indecent dance and gestures, sometimes unclothing themselves; others who have no true profession but act as vagabonds telling scandalous tales; and those who play instruments for the delectation of men and act out the gestes of princes and the lives of saints.'

He left no doubt in Petysance's mind how he classified de Askeles's troupe, due to perform in front of his church, compared to the low mob cavorting in front of the priest's. Petysance thought to remind the Prior of the waning powers of the relics of St Frideswide, and the great strength of those of St Eldad. But the old man had retreated into the milling crowd, so he contented himself with cursing his departing back. He continued to watch the secular drama depicted by the puppeteer, but somehow the tart comment from the Prior had spoiled it, and he drifted away. His attention was caught by an ugly man dressed in garish clothes of yellow and green, slashed on the torso to reveal grubby white linen beneath. The juggler had just laid down the plate he had been spinning on a stick and was proclaiming he could perform miracles with a pitcher of water. Curious, the priest hurried over to the crowd he was drawing.

* * *

Thomas de Cantilupe had thought when he left Oxford a few years before that he would never have to suffer the persistent attentions of this particular regent master again. He had almost forgotten how William Falconer could not be diverted from a logical train of thought once he had embarked upon it. He had nearly wiped from his memory the tenacity of the man's importunate demands. Now all those things came flooding back from the past. Before him stood Regent Master Falconer, a little more grizzled about the hair, a little more wrinkled about the face, but for all that the same man. It came as no surprise that he was involved in investigating the death of the monk — he had poked his nose into every suspicious death when de Cantilupe had last been in Oxford. And now he was demanding again. But this time what he was asking was impossible. De Cantilupe had only just reestablished himself in the favour of the King, and Falconer wanted him to put that at risk.

'I cannot do it.'

'But it would take little effort on the part of a man of your wit and wisdom.'

The same old flattery. The trouble was, he responded to it. When Falconer had turned up at the Chancellor's lodgings, along with the youth who now sat quietly in the corner, apparently awed by those in whose presence he sat, de Cantilupe knew he would end up doing exactly what the regent master required. He silently cursed himself for not giving the man's name to the King along with the other supposed conspirators. He had only stopped short out of some insane sense of admiration for the man's tenacity. Even then he had guessed he was going to regret missing the opportunity; now he was sure of it. Still, he tried to avoid the inevitable.

'The King may not be of a mind to allow such frivolity.'

Falconer smiled, leaning forward in his seat to press his great ham of a fist on de Cantilupe's knee. The action was of one recommending a humorous jest to a friend. 'Henry will be happy to please his court at Christmastide, and besides, it is an old custom that the monarch should preserve. It will be the occasion of much jollity, after all.'

De Cantilupe did not think the King thought in terms of bringing 'jollity' to those who fawned on him. He began to speak, but Falconer's grip on the ex-Chancellor's knee tightened.

'And it will give you an opportunity to clear your conscience over those unfortunate burghers, who have done nothing wrong other than offer some imagined slight in the minds of their accusers. You will have reinstated yourself in the King's favour at no cost to anyone.'

De Cantilupe was clearly weakening. He sank back in his chair, gazing at his old adversary. Further resistance was useless — the man always had an answer, and de Cantilupe had always given in. It was folly to think the passage of years would have changed anything. Weirdly, he realized he almost enjoyed their exchanges.

'Very well. I will suggest to the King that he elect a Lord of Misrule from his kitchen servants at the feast today. I will do my best to ensure that . . .' He looked enquiringly at the youth.

'Thomas.' Falconer motioned for Thomas Symon to come forward.

'That Thomas, here, becomes that Lord. But after that it is up to the boy.'

Falconer clapped his rough hands together in delight and smiled at the student before him. Thomas grinned back confidently — he had helped his master before with similar machinations.

'Excellent. Thomas knows exactly what to do.'

* * *

When Stefano de Askeles heard that John Peper had been led off by the constable to be incarcerated for the murder of the unfortunate monk, he was furious. Not that he cared for the life of his actor, nor for the loss of his acting skills, for truly the man was poor at his craft. But his imprisonment left him short of a Noah and all the other minor parts that Peper played in the cycle. And no one would be able to learn them in time. Besides, the man was privy to a secret that de Askeles would rather he kept. In prison he might have occasion to blurt it out.

The evening shadows lengthened across the courtyard, and with the torches extinguished the stage lacked its normal glitter. Long and ominous shadows were cast by the device that the Prior's carpenters had only just installed at the back of the stage. With solid uprights and a sturdy crossbeam from which hung ropes threaded through pulleys, the device more nearly resembled a gallows than what in fact it was: the means by which God's throne, attached to the ropes and by the hidden effort of several brawny men, would appear to ascend uncannily to the heavens at the end of the play cycle. Now to de Askeles's eyes the gilded Mansion of God was dulled and without lustre. He sat on the edge of the platform drumming his leather-clad heels on its upright face and clutching his fur-lined robe around him against the cold of the evening.

With the performances now barely more than a day away, and an indication that the King might attend, he was boiling with anger that all was not going well. If only he could secure the release of John Peper, then there was every opportunity to impress the royal court, and perhaps even earn a lucrative living from being taken into the King's employ. Of course he could then be rid of Peper, and Will Plome and Agnes Cheke as well. They were of use to fill a costume, or entertain stupid peasants, but at the King's court he would need finer players. Players like Margaret Peper, who was the finest saltatore he had ever seen. Her lithe and shapely limbs would be the currency to buy the cooperation of any courtier he fancied to further his aims. And all this was threatened by the stupidity of the woman's husband. It wasn't even as if he could have killed the monk. He slammed his fists down on the floor of the stage, causing an echo to boom through the darkness.

'Who's there?'

A tremulous voice drifted out of the darkness at the side of the stage. De Askeles recognized it for the voice of the troupe's palmist and soothsayer, Agnes Cheke. At another time he might have taken the opportunity to play a trick on her, working on her fear of the place where but recently a man had been murdered. But another idea had begun to form in his mind. He sprang to his feet, and called out, 'It's only me, you stupid woman. Stop skulking in the dark and come here.'

Agnes's courage returned when she realized it was neither the spirit of the monk nor the substance of his murderer that had caused the noise. She stomped over to confront him. 'I'll thank you not to call me stupid.'

De Askeles ignored her retort and grasped her arm, drawing her to the flickering light of the tallow lamp he had left on the front of the stage.

'What did you tell the constable when he asked where you were when the monk was murdered?'

'The truth, of course. What did you tell him?'

Once again de Askeles brushed aside her comment, and pressed his face close up to hers, his breath blowing frosty clouds at her. 'Were you on your own? Did you tell him you were alone?'

'Yes I was, and I told him so. I was washing those angels' robes that got dirty when the robbers attacked us. I was in the courtyard behind the inn.'

'So no one else saw you there?'

'I don't think so. Why do you want to know?'

De Askeles grinned with pleasure at his own cleverness. 'Because you are going to tell the constable that you lied.'

Agnes began to protest, but de Askeles clapped his hand across her mouth, stifling her comment.

'You are going to tell him you were with John Peper. And I don't care if you say he helped you wash the robes, or he got between your legs. Just convince him that John couldn't have killed the monk.' He released the grip on her mouth, and she began to protest. But he stopped her. 'You do want to help him, don't you?'

Agnes was puzzled at first by de Askeles's apparent solicitude. She had imagined he would be glad to be rid of John, so that he could do whatever he liked with Margaret. Getting him released would not help that. On the other hand, he probably just wanted to make sure the plays went well the day after tomorrow. And why should she object? She was a fool not to have thought of the idea herself. She shrugged de Askeles's hands from her shoulders and agreed to do as he asked.

'I'm not going to say he bedded me, mind.' She blushed at the thought, and de Askeles roared with laughter at her obvious discomfiture.

'You're right. No one would believe that a man would fancy you. So you'd better tell him something else — just be convincing.'

He jumped down from the stage and strode away towards the wagon, knocking the guttering tallow lamp off the edge of the stage and leaving Agnes in the icy darkness.

* * *

After persuading de Cantilupe to his mind, William Falconer felt he had done all he could for the moment in prosecuting his search for Roger Bacon's alchemist. Zerach's release depended on the plan he had devised to get Thomas Symon elected as the Lord of Misrule at the King's court, and Henry's willingness to play the foolish traditional Christmas game. Falconer's mind now turned back to the murder on the troubadours' stage. He wondered how far Peter Bullock had got with his investigations. His old friend was a sound keeper of the peace, good at knocking foolish heads together and resolving domestic quarrels. But when it came to navigating the convolutions of a murder, he feared Peter's directness blinded him to the narrow alley where the guilty often lurked. He trod only the seductively broad highway that could often mislead.

As he crossed Fish Street on his way to Bullock's home at the foot of the Great Keep, Falconer spotted a commotion at the door to Jehozadok's house and teaching school. He fished in the purse at his waist, pulled out his eye-lenses and held the device to his face. The bustle of the lane swam into focus. He made out a knot of young Jews, at the centre of which was a hot-headed youth he knew by the name of Deulegard. They stood on the steps up to the school, surrounding an older Jew who was vaguely familiar to Falconer. The old man was dressed in fine clothes, and was clearly a wealthy man. Falconer recognized him as an elder in the Jewish community, but an ineffectual one when it came to being decisive. He seemed reluctant to let them enter the building, but his wrinkled face showed fear and he was clearly going to back down. As Falconer approached, Deulegard finally bundled the old man out of the way and stormed in through the door, followed by the rest of the angry group.

The elder scurried away at the sight of Falconer, casting a fearful look over his shoulder. At the door, now firmly closed to the activities of the lane, the regent master knocked loudly, wondering if Jehozadok needed his assistance. The sound of raised voices behind the solid oak ceased, the door was opened and Deulegard's face appeared in the crack.

'What do you want?' The youth's voice was taut with anger.

'I wanted to speak with my friend the rabbi.'

'You can't see him.'

Falconer tried to protest, but his comments were abruptly cut off.

'It is not convenient now. He is teaching.'

Falconer's massive hand grabbed the edge of the door as the youth tried to close it on him. He was about to force an entry when a piping, reedy voice made itself heard.

'Do not worry, my old friend, I will see you later. For the moment I have a little business to attend to.'

Deulegard allowed the door to open wider, and Falconer was surprised to see the frail old rabbi standing in the passage leading from the front door. He was leaning on the arm of one of the youths who had rushed into the school. Together they looked like a gnarled and ancient tree stump shattered by lightning out of which rose a new and whippy sapling. Falconer had not seen Jehozadok outside his bedchamber for several months, and this more than the odd events on the doorstep alarmed him even further. However, the old man had clearly recognized his voice, and now he smiled at him, urging him with a look to be patient.

'I will explain to you later. But now I have to deal with these hotheads myself.'

'Very well.'

Falconer stepped back and, though still fearful for his friend's safety, allowed Deulegard to slam the door in his face.

* * *

Jehozadok might have been frail, but he was still a commanding figure to some of those who stood around him. His old eyes roamed over the knot of agitated youths, all dressed in the dull garb that was the only clothing allowed the King's Jews. Not that they were the King's property now — some years had passed since Henry had sold them to his younger brother, Richard of Cornwall, for a handsome profit. There was Cressant, the youngster who had had the courtesy to support him, Jose, Aaron son of Elias, Aaron son of Isaac, Samuel, Bonamy, and Deulegard — sons and grandsons of fathers he had taught. These young men now studied the religious texts with the rabbi themselves but were not so bound by the careful ways of their elders. Years of persecution had led Jehozadok's generation to take care in their dealings with Christians, and to keep themselves very much to themselves. Deulegard and his friends were of an age to be frustrated by this narrow confinement.

Jehozadok's gaze alighted on the ringleader of the group as he slammed the door on the rabbi's trusted Christian friend. He almost wished he could discuss the present problem with Falconer, but perhaps even he would not truly understand. Deulegard paced agitatedly up and down the narrow hallway, his fists tightening on some imagined adversary. Jehozadok sought to calm him.

'Never fear, we will take action.'

Deulegard's face screwed up in fury. 'And what do you propose to do, when we don't even know who did it?'

'I will find out who it was.'

Deulegard was unconvinced. He pressed his nose close up to the wrinkled face of the old man. 'How? Solomon is dead. Can he speak to you from the grave?'

Jehozadok knew what he was about to say would only irritate the youth, but he could not help himself. The boy needed teaching a lesson. 'He spoke to me some time before he died and told me something quite interesting. He told me he saw God.'

Deulegard snorted in contempt. 'This is nonsense. Anyway, I don't care who killed him for the moment. It was a Christian, so any Christian will suit our purpose. They all need teaching a lesson. Tomorrow the priest will parade his holy relic in front of the mob. That's when we should act. Or during their stupid plays.'

Jehozadok paled at the thought and began to protest. But his control over these hotheads was fading with his sight. Deulegard had delivered a focus for their pent-up frustrations and they grasped it greedily. For once the old man had misjudged and lost the argument to blind anger. Before he could protest further, all but Cressant surrounded Deulegard and clapped him on the back. They would deal a blow for their race tomorrow. In the meantime, the youths left the Scola in twos and threes, still mindful of their precarious position in English society. Only one youth, Cressant, hung back, and looked at Jehozadok with guilty eyes. He touched the old man's arm.

'Don't worry. It will be all right.'

'I somehow don't think so.'

Jehozadok's prophecy was spoken to the youth's retreating back.

* * *

'You've arrested John Peper!'

Peter Bullock's face fell at Falconer's reaction to his announcement. He had felt sure that his old friend would be proud of his deductive powers. Why, hadn't the man agreed the culprit was John Peper when last they had spoken? Bullock could not stop himself from reminding Falconer of this. The regent master frowned.

'Did I? I do not remember that — are you sure you understood me correctly?' He paused, seeing the thunder-clouds of anger crossing his friend's face. 'Oh well, I suppose you must be right.'

Bullock's smile of self-satisfaction returned, and he started to pour more good ale into Falconer's empty mug.

'However, I was distracted by the errand that Roger Bacon had set me, and no doubt was not thinking straight. Did I not also remind you to check on the carpenter?'

The flow of ale stopped abruptly as Bullock tensed. His friend could be so condescending. He could not accept that someone other than himself might uncover the murderer.

'The carpenter does not matter. You see, the scene before Peper tried to kill de Askeles was the Flood. As Noah, Peper was actually going to build an ark. He had a bag full of carpenter's tools in his hands.'

Falconer raised his mug, and saluted the constable. 'Then I congratulate you on solving the murder.'

A woman's voice cut across their good humour. 'I think you should hear me out before you get too drunk with your success.'

Agnes Cheke stood in the doorway of Bullock's spartan chamber.

CHAPTER ELEVEN

DEVIL: Now see whither thou hast us brought
To a dungeon, small path to trace.
All this sorrow 'tis thou hast sought,
The Devil speed thy stinking face!

The Fall of Lucifer

The morning dawned cold and clear, which pleased Stefano de Askeles greatly. It took all day to present the play cycle, and the size of the acting troupe's purse depended on the size of the crowd. And the size of the crowd depended on the weather. Though he had drunk heavily the night before, he woke up early feeling invigorated. A performance day always acted on his constitution in this way. He felt doubly pleased because Agnes had returned the previous night with the sullen John Peper in tow. The man had not had the good grace even to thank de Askeles for saving him, but merely slunk off to his bed. Agnes had briefly explained that she had convinced the constable that John had been with her at the crucial moment, though she did not explain how she had done so. Then she too retired to her solitary mattress, leaving de Askeles to carouse alone.

He rose from his warm bed in the Golden Ball Inn, collected the bowl of water left outside his door and dashed the icy liquid on his face. He drew his wet fingers through his long golden locks and dressed quickly. From the corner of his room the gilded mask of God, the face set in a sunburst, eyelessly observed his every move. This was going to be a good day.

* * *

It was not a good morning for Peter Bullock. It still rankled that he had had to release Peper the previous night. And what is more, Falconer had been present to witness his discomfiture. When Agnes Cheke had interrupted their drinking session, he asked her what she meant.

'I mean that John could not be your murderer. He was with me when the killer struck.'

'But you told me you were alone when the murder took place.'

'I was . . . for a while. Then John joined me.'

Bullock groaned and looked despairingly across the table at his friend. Falconer's face was impassive as he swivelled on the bench to face the woman. He motioned her forward, and she came and sat at the opposite end of the bench.

'Let's start again. Where were you when the rehearsals started?'

Agnes pointed at the constable. 'Where I told him. I was washing out some costumes in the yard of the Golden Ball.'

'Did anyone see you there?'

Agnes's response was almost too quick. 'No one.'

'Except John Peper,' corrected Falconer.

Agnes dropped her head momentarily, then looked Falconer firmly in the eye. 'I thought you meant before John came.'

'So you were washing costumes, and then John arrived. How do you know it was not after the murder had taken place?'

'Well, I can't be sure. But he said he had just finished Noah and had come back to see if Margaret was at the inn.

Herod and the Slaying of the Innocents is close to the end of the cycle — you recall they were rehearsing it in the dark.'

She turned to Falconer for confirmation. 'When John found me, there was still some light in the sky. And we sat in the yard for quite some while before someone came and told us an actor had been killed on stage. I was telling John's future.'

'His future?' Falconer was puzzled.

Bullock smiled and explained. 'Agnes reads palms.'

Falconer frowned but nodded his head at Agnes and begged her to continue.

'Well, that's all, really. We went back to the church and found you all there.' Agnes leaned back, her palms on the edge of the table, as though she had just completed an Herculean task. Bullock shook his head in disbelief. He had incarcerated the wrong man. Only one thought struck him, and he narrowed his eyes.

'Why didn't Peper tell me he was with you when I asked him?'

Agnes looked down at her lap. 'He . . . was embarrassed. The rest of the troupe think my palmistry is just for yokels.'

Bullock's face reddened at the thought of Agnes reading his palm the other day.

'But John believes that there is truth in it . . . as I do,' she added, realizing why the constable looked so uncomfortable. 'He didn't want anyone to know where he was and why.'

'How do I know you are not lying to save his neck?'

'You could get Peper to confirm the story,' suggested Falconer, stretching back on his seat. Bullock grunted and pushed himself up on to his feet. He picked up the huge bunch of keys that lay between them on the table and told Agnes to follow him. Falconer stayed by the fire, an amused look on his face.

When the glum constable returned, with neither Agnes nor Peper in tow, he found Falconer holding his fusty robes spread out before the fire in the hearth. There was a smile on his face, which annoyed Bullock.

'I don't know why you are so cheerful. Unless you like seeing me being made a fool of?'

Falconer strode forward and gripped his friend's arm. 'Of course I don't. But now you've released Peper we can begin the investigation properly.'

Bullock groaned inwardly at the word *we* — Falconer obviously could not keep away from the murder any longer. Bullock had been lucky he had not interfered before now. Though, bearing in mind the error he had made, perhaps he should be grateful that his old friend was now showing interest.

'Of course, I do not believe a word of what we have just been told.'

Bullock was astonished. 'But he confirmed what she said.'

'In what order?'

Bullock did not understand, so Falconer asked him to relate what had happened.

'I took Agnes down to the cell, opened it up, and asked Peper if he had been with her when the murder took place. He took one look at her, said he was, and I let them go.'

Falconer shook his head in despair. 'Don't you see you told him in advance what Agnes wanted him to confirm? You still don't know the truth.'

'Then why did you allow me to let Peper go?' He lurched up from his seat, scattering the dirty platters from which he had consumed his frugal breakfast. 'I must stop them both immediately.'

Falconer restrained his impulsive friend. 'Steady, Peter. I said I did not believe what Agnes told us. That does not mean I believe John Peper to be guilty. Or necessarily innocent. But I would like to know why Agnes chose to lie, and where Peper really was when the murder took place. Those little truths may help us to build a picture of the greater truth.'

For Bullock the bewildering convolutions of Falconer's thinking had begun again.

* * *

The King was in great good humour for he was winning at dice. His opponents, Roger Mortimer and Thomas de Cantilupe, and he were drawn closely round a table from which the breakfast meal had recently been cleared. The wine goblets of the two visitors were being replenished with alacrity by Henry's steward, and their faces were flushed. Henry was an abstemious man and knew the value of a clear head when gaming — the one indulgence he allowed his pious soul.

'Inn and Inn!' cried Henry, as he cast two sixes and two threes with the four dice. Both the other men groaned as the King scooped up the pile of gold coins with his slender fingers. He drew them to the growing heap at his elbow and picked one coin from his winnings. He cast it in the centre of the table where it rang against the oak surface.

'I wager on my throw.'

Mortimer and de Cantilupe, great men though they were, could ill afford the money they were losing. But the King was enjoying himself, and nothing was to stand in his way. After all it was Christmastide, and the King in good humour could be a king who would grant requests. The two men threw their coins on to the table, and the King shook the four dice in the wooden cup. With a cry of encouragement he threw them on the table, then stared in disbelief at the numbers that lay uppermost. A six, a four, a two and a one — he had thrown an Out and owed both of his competitors the wager on the table.

Mortimer smirked but hid his satisfaction in the wine goblet he raised to his lips. Grumbling under his breath, the King counted out an equal measure of coins for both men. As the servant at his elbow refilled his goblet, de Cantilupe picked the money off the table and was surprised to feel the youth's hip nudge his shoulder. Turning to the miscreant, he was about to reprimand the clumsy oaf when he realized it was Falconer's accomplice, Thomas Symon. The youth was grinning at him and casting his eyes towards the King. Damn his impertinence — he was pressing the former Chancellor to initiate the plan agreed with Falconer. De Cantilupe needed to be the judge of when, and the King must at least be winning again before he tried. He motioned with his hand below the table to tell the boy to be patient.

'My turn, I believe,' he said and scooped up the recalcitrant dice. The wager made, he rattled the dice vigorously in their cup, praying that he would lose. Shaking them out on the surface he was relieved to see only one doublet — a pair of twos. It was a single Inn, and no one won the pot. The money stayed in the centre of the table and the next round's wagers were added to it. Shake and toss. Two fours, another single Inn. The sweat poured from de Cantilupe's forehead as with trembling fingers he added the last of his coins to the pot and returned the four dice to the cup. It was now or never, and his prayers ascended to the heavens. He closed his eyes tight and threw the dice on to the table.

The King roared, and de Cantilupe fearfully opened one eye. Another Out — he had lost and the King had won.

'You are not cut out for gaming, my dear Thomas,' chortled Henry as he gathered in the pile of coins all to himself, before de Cantilupe could share them out. 'And how do you propose to pay Mortimer what you owe him?'

'I fear he will have to wait until I have pawned my last pair of boots, Your Majesty.'

'And then you can be a barefoot minorite, begging for your keep.'

The King roared with laughter at his jest, and his two companions joined in. Glancing over his shoulder at the youth who still stood at the edge of his vision, de Cantilupe coughed nervously and spoke.

'The first thing that this poor friar begs is that you elect a Lord of Misrule for Christmas. It is a long tradition in the halls of Oxford.'

The King ceased laughing and frowned. 'A Lord of Misrule?' He toyed with the pile of coins before him as he turned de Cantilupe's suggestion over in his mind. He fixed his eyes on the ex-Chancellor, his left eyelid appearing to wink at him in approval. De Cantilupe held his breath. Suddenly the King crashed his palm down flat upon the table, causing the coins to leap in the air.

'A wonderful idea. He can lead our procession to the play cycle this very day.'

Mortimer and de Cantilupe grinned and raised their goblets in salute.

'Whom shall I choose?'

Mortimer was about to speak, but de Cantilupe beat him to it. 'Why, the first lowly servant you come across.' He grabbed Thomas's arm. 'Why not this young oaf? He looks poor enough.'

Thomas was a little offended, for he had worn his best clothes, albeit patched at the elbow and torn at the waist. But, swallowing his pride, he pretended to cringe at being dragged to the fore in such exalted company. Indeed, he did not need to pretend very hard for his heart was beating thunderously at being brought under the King's gaze.

'What's your name, boy?'

'T-Thomas, Your Majesty.'

The King smiled broadly. 'How auspicious — he shares your name, de Cantilupe. Thomas will be our Lord for the day.'

The King performed a low and exaggerated bow before the startled Thomas. His grey beard almost touched the floor as he begged the new Lord to give his first orders. The boy gazed round the room, wondering how he should lead up to what he wanted from Henry. Despite the King's show of obsequiousness, Thomas did not think he would respond well to being treated as a servant, or to being given too outrageous a command too soon. No, he would build up to what Master Falconer wanted him to ask. Thomas pointed an imperious finger at Roger Mortimer.

'You. Fetch me wine, and quickly.'

The haughty baron was about to protest when he saw that Henry was mightily amused, and, forcing a grin on to his thunderous features, he bowed and left the King's chamber. De Cantilupe cast Thomas a warning glance, for he knew that Mortimer was a resentful man, and did not forget a slight easily. But the student lord did not see him, because Henry was leading him towards the heavy, ornate chair that the King of England reserved for himself. He placed Thomas firmly on the throne and laughed.

'You have clearly given me a lesson in how to handle my unruly barons. Perhaps if I had treated de Montfort as a slave, he would not have risen against me. Now you must have the finest robes we can find — for a Lord cannot be seen to be shabbily dressed.'

Thomas wriggled with pleasure, almost forgetting what he was about, and his instructions from Master William Falconer.

* * *

Falconer, meanwhile, was in search of a carpenter. He had no proof that it was the original owner of the murderous chisel who had killed the monk, but there was no harm in discovering the man's identity and seeing if he bore de Askeles a grudge. He began in the north-west quarter of the city, where those who belonged to the carpenters' guild resided. The neat and orderly nature of the houses spoke not only of the skill of those who lived there, but also of the wealth that their work generated. A skillful carpenter was valued and could earn three pence a day, where Falconer's own stipend for lecturing was twelve pence a year. Those who had money — landowners, merchants and princes of the Church — paid well for a skilled artisan. The Prior of St Frideswide was no exception.

Having no other method than knocking on doors at random, Falconer at first thought he had been lucky to find a carpenter who had worked on the players' stage at the very first house he approached. When he tried another and another and was successful everywhere he went, he realized that the good Prior had employed nearly every tradesman in the city. He showed each man the chisel he had pulled from the body of Brother Adam. Each man, mindful of the implications, denied flatly that the tool was his. Several were eager to show Falconer their bag of tools and demonstrate that they still possessed a chisel of the very shape and size of the one in Falconer's hands. None had a chisel missing.

Only when he was about to give up the fruitless search did he glean a useful piece of information. The pinched face of the man at the last house he tried contorted in a sneer as he took the chisel from Falconer's open palm.

'This is Ralph's.'

Falconer was excited, but puzzled. 'How do you know?'

The man twisted the chisel round in his horny hands and pointed to the shoulder of the metal blade.

'Look here — there's his mark. He didn't trust anyone not to steal his damn tools and marked them all with his initials.'

Falconer peered closely at the blade — his short-sightedness working to his advantage for once — and saw in the width of the chisel, not on its surface where he might have expected a mark of ownership, a neat R.

'Where might I find this Ralph?'

'Now that's a good question.'

The answer had brought the regent master not to another well-to-do residence in the carpenters' quarter, but to the hovels that huddled outside South Gate. He stepped with caution along one of the warrens that meandered through the mean shanties which leaned for support one on the other. The scrawny pigs that snuffled through the earth at his feet warned Falconer that he was probably walking through a midden rather than a street. Suspicious eyes peered out from gloomy doorways that often had no greater means of security than a strip of tattered sacking. These people were at the bottom of the social heap, and Falconer wondered why Ralph should be found here. The man who had guided him here had paid grudging tribute to the man's skills as a carpenter. Then why was he in such poor surroundings?

The pinched-faced carpenter had said that Falconer could find what he sought at the end of this meanest of all alleys. The hovel before him did at least possess a door, though it looked as if it had seen better days on a pigsty before it graced this opening. He tapped gently on it for fear it might collapse. The sound of noisy children behind it was silenced before the door was opened a crack, and a woman's face appeared in the gap. She was attractive, and too fair of face to have been in this stew for long. The other faces Falconer had seen were thin, drawn and wrinkled, all seemingly of advanced years though some must have hidden younger souls. This woman's eyes were swollen as though she had been weeping for a long time and had but recently ceased. She clearly could not trust her voice to speak without causing a fresh flood of tears, and simply stared at Falconer, a question in her red-rimmed eyes.

'I am looking for a carpenter called Ralph. I was told he lived here.'

Tears welled in the woman's eyes but no confirmation escaped her lips. She simply turned away from Falconer and disappeared into the gloomy interior, leaving the door ajar. Falconer pushed it open and stepped over the threshold. Once his eyes had adjusted to the dark, he realized the single room that stood behind the unpromising exterior was as neat and tidy as it could possibly be in such straitened circumstances. The furniture was old and worn, but the table remained scrubbed and clean — telling of a woman who strove to maintain some semblance of a former good life.

'If you want to take something in lieu of debt, you will see that there is precious little left.'

The woman stood at the back of the room, two scared children huddled into the patched gown that hung off her slender frame. They all looked afraid.

'I am not here to take anything from you,' said Falconer in his gentlest tones. 'I merely wished to talk to your husband. If you are Ralph's wife, that is.'

There was a momentary glint of hope in the woman's eyes.

'Have you got some work for him? He is an excellent worker — please don't judge us by these surroundings. This is just . . . temporary.'

Falconer sighed. He knew from the pinched-faced man that Ralph had indeed once been a good carpenter, but he was also a good drinker. Lately, his work had got worse and worse as he drank more and more. What little he earned barely paid for his ale now, and he had failed to pay his rent. The consequence had been what Falconer now saw for himself. The woman realized from the regent master's hesitation that he knew her situation, and the optimism drained from her face. Her voice trembled as she spoke.

'You will probably find him drinking away what little the Prior paid him at Kepeharm's inn. Either that or sleeping it off in some midden somewhere. We have not seen him for days.'

Falconer thanked her courteously and closed the rickety door on the tableau of three destitute souls brought down by one man's weakness. He resolved to remain sober this Christmastide. As he reentered the city through the lofty arch of South Gate, he realized that he had not thought to ask the woman if he could have a look at Ralph's tools. He could at least have verified the other carpenter's claim that the murder weapon had belonged to Ralph. But then the uproar that confronted him on Fish Street drove all such thoughts from his mind.

CHAPTER TWELVE

DEVIL: Thou hast brought us all this wicked way
With all thy might and pride,
Away from bliss that would lust for aye
In sorrow ever more here to abide.

The Fall of Lucifer

Uproar hardly described it — it had been close to a full-scale riot. As Falconer heard it from Peter Bullock later, it had all begun around midday.

'They knew Petysance was going to lead a procession around the town showing off that relic and must have planned it. Though God knows why.'

The priest of St Aldate's plan was to process his new acquisition — the holy arm-bone of St Eldad — along the High Street, down Shidyerd Street and back to his church past St Frideswide's. This last port of call would seem to have been the prime purpose of the route. The procession was timed to pass St Frideswide's just as most citizens were gathering to find a favourable vantage point for the mystery plays. The procession consisted of several minor members of the clergy who served under Edward Petysance, all clad in their best robes with the gold thread glittering in the watery sun and following the cross that graced St Aldate's altar. Before the bearer of the ornate silver cross strode Petysance himself, clutching to his chest the new metal-bound box that held the relic. The box lay on a white linen sheet that covered his arms so that he did not soil the wood that touched the relic with his bare hands. The effect was dramatic, and many folk were drawn away from the courtyard of St Frideswide's to gawk at the procession as it passed. The smug look on the priest's face at seeing this triumph was soon to be wiped off, however.

The sequence of events as the procession emerged into Fish Street was confused, but everyone agreed they had first heard Talmudic chants emanating from the upper rooms along the street. At first no one took any notice of this, except to be mildly irritated. The Jews often practised their rituals behind closed doors, and good Christian voices always drowned the chanting out. If not, a judicious stone lobbed through an upper floor window usually had a similar effect. This time it was not to be.

From what Bullock could make out from those he questioned after the event, several young Jews spilled out from the Scola almost opposite St Aldate's Church and scattered the startled crowd before them. The good peasants of Oxford were more used to giving Jews knocks than receiving them from that quarter and fell back as the mob of youths advanced down the crowded street. A few jeers were cast at their black-clad backs, but nothing that would occasion the violence that followed.

Others questioned, saw the group of Jews apparently on a collision course with Petysance's procession, and could only gaze in disbelief as the fanatical mob bore down on the clergy and rained blows on them. At the head of the procession, everyone saw Edward Petysance wrestling with one of the youths over the holy relic. Indeed, the bulky box seemed to be the goal of the Jews. The white-faced priest had hold of one end, the Jew the other, the white linen cloth having slipped into the sewage channel that ran at their feet. Two of the Jews grappled with the bearer of the holy cross, while the others rolled on the ground with those who made up the rest of the procession, preventing them from assisting Petysance. For a moment it had appeared that the priest was losing this grotesque tug-of-war, until the unthinkable happened. The cross-bearer could no longer hold the heavy silver cross aloft and beat off the two who attacked him at the same time. He swung the object like a weapon, cracking open the skull of one of his attackers, who staggered off bleeding from his wound. Unfortunately the force of the swing caused the cross to slip from the clergyman's hands and it plunged into the channel of ordure where the linen cloth lay. The defilement of such a sacred object brought a single gasp from the crowd, who until then had stood and watched the extraordinary sight of Jews attacking Christians openly in the street. The cross lay dirtied and broken in the filth.

With a snarl several men in the crowd leapt to the aid of the clergy. As the Jew who grappled with Petysance hesitated, the priest snatched the box from his grasp and scuttled into the protection of the onlookers. The other Jews looked at their ringleader, then as one made off through a gap in the crowd, blows raining on their backs. All but one made the safety of the Scola, from whose steps Deulegard yelled a warning. 'This is not the end of it. A life for a life.'

He was dragged in by his comrades and the heavy doors closed abruptly. Too stunned to be aware of the danger he was in, the unfortunate youth whose head was already cracked lay prostrate in the remains of the vegetable stall against which he had fallen, and the anger of those present was assuaged by raining blows upon his helpless form. Aaron, son of Isaac, was dead before Peter Bullock could force his way through the crowd.

'This will be nothing but trouble for me,' grumbled the constable. 'Like it or not, I am paid to protect the Jews. Then they do something like that. This dead youth will be a source of claim and counter-claim for weeks to come.'

'Thoughtless of him to get himself clubbed to death.' Falconer's response was tart — he still could not accept his friend's disregard for the life of the Jews in their midst, even though it was a dislike shared by most of Christendom. Bullock recognized the uncertain ground on which he was treading and sought to mollify his comrade.

'At least no one else was hurt. No doubt the Church will demand some reparation in the form of money, and all will be back to normal. The sooner the better as far as I am concerned, though I worry about the threat of further trouble. A life for a life — I wonder what he meant?' He shrugged his bowed shoulders. 'Good job the plays are due to start — that diverted a lot of people's attention away from further mayhem. Are you going to watch them?'

Falconer roused himself from deep thoughts. 'What? Oh — the plays cycle. Perhaps later. I have other matters to attend to first.'

The constable knew better than to ask what matters they were. He wanted to go and see the plays and didn't want to be held up as Falconer expounded fanciful theories implicating the actors' monkey, the Archangel Gabriel, and for all he knew God himself in the recent mayhem and death.

* * *

Falconer was glad that most folk had gone to watch the plays as he swung his long legs over the wall that ran part of the length of Jewry Lane. He bunched his grubby robe up between his thighs and dropped on to the soft earth of the rear yard of the first house on Fish Street. He had learned of this back way into the Fish Street shops from an impoverished student at Aristotle's Hall who supplemented his meagre allowance by stealing from the traders who occupied the ground floors of the houses. Peter Bullock had caught him in the act and brought him to Regent Master Falconer for punishment. The youth had regretted his dishonesty for as long as his back continued to ache. When he had been caught a second time, Falconer had expelled him. No doubt he had ended up as a wandering goliard as many failed or lazy students did, earning a few coins by singing in taverns and at fairs. There were probably several in the entertainers who thronged Oxford at this moment.

But now Falconer was grateful for the youth's knowledge. If you could get to the back of the shops this way, then you could reach the rear of the Scola. And having assumed the front doors would be firmly closed to all Christians, including himself, Falconer had decided to try their back door. He scrambled over the next stout wooden fence as he made his way along the backs. His feet landed in something soft and warm, and he cursed as the familiar farmyard stench of pig dung rose to his nostrils. His boots were so worn that he did not doubt the ordure was already seeping through the cracks — he would not be rid of the smell for weeks. His weak eyes made out a rusty-coloured hump at the back of the yard — the smell of urine and deep snuffling noises informed him that the depositor of the dung was loose, and probably angry at being disturbed. There was a student legend of a youth who preserved his life when attacked by a wild boar by stuffing his copy of Aristotle in the beast's mouth. The regent master in Falconer had always thought it a waste of a good text. In any case, he did not have a book with him at present, so he could not emulate the deed. He quickly hopped over the next wall, leaving the squeals of the irate pig behind him. Landing awkwardly, he was on his hands and knees when a solemn voice spoke.

'A rather unorthodox arrival, my friend. But then you never take the easy route to your goal, do you?' The aged Rabbi Jehozadok stood over the crestfallen Falconer, leaning heavily on a stout stick. 'I would offer a hand to you, but I fear it would be of no assistance.'

Falconer waved away the apology and got to his feet, attempting to wipe the stains of his journey from his already dowdy robe. The old man could barely see Falconer and the state he was in, but his nose told him the full story.

'I see you have encountered our good neighbour — his habits are not of the cleanest.'

'Though I am told they are very intelligent creatures, rabbi.'

Jehozadok frowned. 'Hmm. Still, I am sure you have not . . . er . . . dropped in to discuss the merits of swine. No doubt you want to know the reason for today's little incident, though it is truly none of your business.'

Jehozadok's voice was unusually curt, not at all like his normal measured tones. And he seemed uneasy, casting his unseeing gaze over his shoulder at the stone steps leading to the upper rooms where he lived. Falconer thought he saw a youth hovering in the shadows, but if he did the onlooker was gone before he could screw up his eyes to see more clearly. Jehozadok continued.

'Well, I suppose I should be grateful that you ask why rather than assuming the worst. They were foolish, but the provocation was great. Come, let us talk inside.' He waved his gnarled hand in a vague invitation. In deference to the old man's finer religious feelings, and his sense of smell, Falconer pulled off his boots, and left them in the yard before assisting the rabbi indoors.

* * *

'Release all prisoners?'

Henry could not believe his ears. This grubby youth dressed in his own purple robes, and ensconced on the throne that travelled everywhere with him, had asked for the release of all prisoners. The King cast his eyes around his courtiers in disbelief. Mortimer was smirking, convinced that the boy had overstepped the mark. De Cantilupe was stony-faced and held his breath, sure that Falconer's ploy to gain the incarcerated merchants their freedom was not going to work. Everyone else present hesitated in the fashion of true courtiers — they waited to see the King's reaction before they committed themselves. For the King the game had been most enjoyable. Having someone else deciding matters and issuing instructions had been unusual for him. The last time it had happened, Simon de Montfort not this youth had been involved, and the circumstances had been much less pleasant. He would not like to lose another war with his barons. No, this was a much more satisfactory way to have decisions made for him. It had cost another battle and many lives to claim his power back from de Montfort, and the ramifications still lived with him in the form of the disinherited and disgruntled knights who were holed up in Ely causing trouble. This youth would be deposed and forgotten when the Christmas revels were over.

In the meantime, he was enjoying the discomfiture to which Mortimer and his other pompous courtiers were being put by the Lord of Misrule. This Thomas was oblivious of the implications of his every action. Had it been the King himself ordering them about in the same way, he would be causing such resentment that it would be inevitably expressed in the future as minor acts of revenge. Henry had not survived fifty years on the throne without being fully attuned to the aspirations and actions of those who surrounded him. He had lived in this stifling atmosphere all his life, and it was second nature to him now.

The boy repeated his request.

'That is what I said. And as Lord of Misrule I expect to be obeyed.'

De Cantilupe raised his eyes to the heavens, thinking that Thomas had gone too far. But the King smiled and bowed low. He was beginning to enjoy this topsy-turvy idea. For the moment at least he felt as though a great burden of decision-making had been lifted from his shoulders.

'So be it. De Cantilupe — go and see to it immediately. In the meantime, we shall prepare to see the Prior's plays at St Frideswide's.'

The former Chancellor hurried off to seek out the gaoler before the King could change his mind.

* * *

The milling crowd in front of St Frideswide's Church cheered as someone they recognized emerged on the stage. The amateur performer, clad in ecclesiastical robes as an angel, blushed and stumbled over his lines, to the amusement of his audience. Someone hooted his derision, but others around the unruly individual hushed him as God and Lucifer stepped forth to do battle. These were the real troubadours and they could weave a magic spell. The dowdy blue curtain behind them seemed to sparkle with stars as the midday sun broke through the clouds and lit up the scene.

God, clad in flowing white robes edged in a multi-coloured band flecked with gold, strode to the centre of the stage and turned his gilded face to the expectant crowd. There was a collective gasp as the sun glittered off the starburst of his features. It was no more than a mask, but as the actor spoke it seemed to come alive, almost revealing the true mystery of God.

'Lucifer, how gave I offence to thee?
You, once my friend, are now my foe.
Of all the angels there was none, you know,
So close to me in all my majesty.
I now say "Fall", till I say "No",
In the pit of Hell evermore to be.'

Lucifer cringed before God's might, his mask a blackened skull with gleaming teeth and curved ram's horns. He spat out a curse, then threw his arms up in mock supplication. The crowd, expecting the Devil to slink off the stage as in previous years, gasped as the ground opened and swallowed Lucifer entirely. Wisps of smoke rose from what was clearly the pit of hell. A few superstitious souls at the front of the audience crossed themselves and backed away from the stage. De Askeles, sweating under the mask of God despite the cold, smirked as his trapdoor in the floor of the stage had its effect. The Prior, and the whole of Oxford, would remember this year's play cycle and the man who wrought it. What a pity the King was not yet here to see it. He strode off stage to an expectant buzz and waved his hand imperiously at John Peper who stood at the side of the stage ready to drop the next painted canvas in place. It depicted the Garden of Eden, and was decorated with representations of good English oaks.

* * *

A scrawny man with a scarred face eased his way through the back of the press of people. He made his way to the front of the crowd where the richer onlookers would inevitably be. Importance and wealth were inextricably mixed — except when it came to parish priests, and for that reason Edward Petysance did not lose the few coins he had. Others were not so lucky. Everyone's gaze was fixed on the stage and the unfolding of the Temptation, agog for more marvels like the disappearance of the Devil into hell. John Stockwell, a silversmith of some repute, turned to his right to comment jocularly on the stocky shape of the man playing Eve, and failed to notice the man with the scarred face slip into the crowd at his left elbow. In a trice Stockwell was relieved of his well-filled purse, and the pickpocket moved inconspicuously on. Further into the crowd, Peter Inge, a seller of fish, returned the smile of a scrawny, raw-faced man who appeared at his side just as the Serpent appeared to Eve. When he looked again the newcomer had gone — he would discover only later that so had his bag of hard-earned coins.

Several emptied pockets later, Cuthbert Gledd, known to his dubious friends and implacable enemies as 'Cutpurse', decided he had earned enough, and began to retreat from the jostling throng of good Oxford citizens. He smiled all over his ruined face, thinking that his long journey from London, where that face was becoming too well known, had been worth it after all. At one time his features had been totally nondescript and he could ply his chosen profession of thief quite inconspicuously. He simply melted into the crowd. But then he had tried to steal from a serjeant-at-arms and had lived to regret it.

Just as he was lifting the soldier's purse, someone in the crowd had jostled his elbow and he had been given away. The brute of a serjeant had closed one fist over Cuthbert's hand, realized what he was about, and used the other to hammer the thief's face into a different shape. Still, Cuthbert could not give up what he did best, indeed the only thing he knew how to do. He simply had to move on when his face became known.

When he saw one particularly stupid-looking yokel at the back of the crowd with a bulging purse hanging from his belt, greed got the better of him. The old hunchback was begging to be robbed, and Cutty would oblige. He stumbled as he passed the man, grabbing his waist for support. Apologizing, he recovered himself, and would have walked away, the purse now in his hand. But a vice-like grip on his neck prevented him from escaping, and the 'old man' held him at arm's length like a mewling puppy. Visions of his last beating swam before his eyes, and he groaned. Then he blanched when he saw the man draw a snaggle-edged sword from a scabbard hidden by his left side.

'Now what's all this?' Cutty gasped. 'Leave go an innocent citizen.'

'Innocent? I've watched you take at least six purses, and then you have the nerve to steal my own. Give them over.'

The old man shook the thief, who yelped and emptied his pockets on the ground. Despite his plight, he still tried to bluff his way to freedom.

'Help me, I'm being robbed,' he squawked. At the back of the crowd a few faces turned to see the unequal struggle, grinned and turned back to the play.

'Perhaps I should introduce myself. Peter Bullock, town constable, at your service.'

Cutty Gledd groaned, convinced that he was fated to spend some considerable time in this yokel's prison. But fate intervened in the form of a grizzle-haired regent master of the university. As Bullock prepared to march the thief to his cell, Falconer hurried over to his friend, a worried frown creasing his normally calm features.

'Peter. I must speak with you. Let this man go — whatever he's done cannot be as important as what I have just learned.'

'But—'

'We must talk. Now.'

Bullock sighed, and released Gledd, pushing him down to his knees. The thief smirked at his salvation, then paled when he saw the constable raising his old sword above his head. Falconer, too, gasped at the apparent summary and violent justice Bullock was about to mete out. Gledd flinched as the sword swept down, then squealed in pain as the flat of the blade hit him squarely across the buttocks. For good measure, Bullock's boot followed where the blade had landed, and helped the thief on his way.

'And don't let me see your ugly face again, or it won't be the flat of my sword you'll feel.'

He watched as the chastised thief scurried away in the direction of Fish Street, and a swift exit from Oxford through the South Gate. Then he turned to the grim-faced Falconer.

'Now what is so important that it disturbs the pleasure of locking up a thief, and my enjoyment of the plays?'

'Destroyed all this world shall be,
Save Noah, his wife and sons three,
And their wives too they take,
To be saved for your sake.'

De Askeles thundered out the words of God, and left the stage to John Peper, nervously clutching his false beard, who was enacting Noah. In the wings, watching her husband, was Margaret Peper. She stood with her weight forward on one leg, her sinuous form outlined against the cloth of her dress. The vivid colours of the full-skirted gown she wore for acrobatics in more sober surroundings than the local inn only served to accentuate her sensuality in Stefano's eyes. He pulled the gilded mask from his head and took a swig of wine from the goblet he kept at the side of the stage. Striding over to where she stood, he pressed up against Margaret's back.

Startled, she wriggled free of his embrace and told him to leave her alone. De Askeles was in no mood to be rebuffed. The plays were progressing well, and he already felt he could be denied nothing. Least of all that which he had taken many times before.

He grabbed the woman's arms and roughly pulled her to him. 'I will have you whenever I wish, or you and your weak-willed husband can go begging in the gutter.'

Hatred for de Askeles and her predicament burned in Margaret's bright green eyes. But she submitted to his embrace, thinking only of how she could be rid of him. It was fateful that at that moment John Peper turned to deliver his lines as Noah to his recalcitrant stage wife, Robert Kemp made up as Mother Noah.

> *'Good wife, do as I thee bid.'*
> *'Heavens! Not till I see more need,*
> *Even though you stand there all day staring.'*

Peper could hardly tear his gaze away from the sight over Robert Kemp's shoulder. The sight of his wife blatantly sinking into the embrace of Stefano de Askeles.

CHAPTER THIRTEEN

LUCIFER: And therefore I shall for his sake
Show mankind great envy
As soon as He can him make
I shall at once him destroy.

The Fall of Lucifer

Fifty years on the throne had given Henry an uncanny ability to be in the right place at the right time. His arrival at St Frideswide's Church coincided with the representation on stage of the Adoration of the Magi. Three worthy merchants of Oxford had paid de Askeles well to be the three kings, and now recited their lines with relish. Kneeling, they prayed for a sign, and at that moment Agnes lit a small block of resin. It flared like a star in the sky, and the crowd gasped again at the effect. While they were still blinded by the sudden light, Simon Godrich, dressed as a priest to represent an angel stepped on to the stage. His appearance thus seemed to be magically out of nowhere, and his plangent voice was used to good effect in welcoming the magi.

'Oh! Rise up all ye kings three,
And come you after me,
Into the land of Judee.'

At that moment there was the sound of horses' hooves thudding on the pounded earth of the courtyard, and murmurings from the back of the crowd. Godrich peered into the darkening corners of the yard, angry at whoever had interrupted the scene. The people seemed to fall to their knees in a wave that ran from the back of the audience to those closest to the stage. Behind them, an old man with dull greying hair and a pointed beard of the same colour was easing his stiff limbs off a massive charger. Several men-at-arms scurried around him, ensuring his insulation from those who knelt on the ground. Inside the ring of soldiers was another horse, from which someone sprang with the suppleness of youth. The whisper that was running through the crowd finally reached the stage — it was King Henry. Abruptly those in full view on the platform also fell to their knees.

Though with head bowed, Simon could still see the King from his raised vantage point. He was puzzled by the attention Henry paid to the youth who accompanied him. The King offered the boy his arm and led him to the rostrum where the Prior of St Frideswide's stood, as though the boy were the King and not Henry. Yet he was too young to be the Prince Edward, who was fully a man already. Henry allowed the youth to precede him up the steps to the seats reserved for the Prior and his retinue, and bowed as he sat down on the very cushion the Prior had placed on the bench for his own comfort.

In the crowd, Falconer grinned broadly as he saw Thomas Symon deferred to by the King, and discomfiting the pompous Prior. His plan must be working — but had the Lord of Misrule already been able to gain the prisoners' release? A voice at his elbow answered his unspoken question.

'They are free. But don't involve me in such a mad scheme again. I feared for my neck from dawn today until now.'

It was de Cantilupe, who looked hot and bothered after hurrying from the gaol, where the released merchants had virtually fallen at his feet in gratitude, to catch up with the King's retinue. He mopped his brow with a linen handkerchief and glared at his old adversary, swearing this was going to be the last time that the man endangered his position. He shivered as the cold of the advancing winter's evening chilled his sweat, and stamped off to join the King. Falconer followed his retreating form, and looked up at the royal group in time to catch an exaggerated wink from Thomas Symon on his lofty perch. The boy waved his arm imperiously, but it was only after the King beside him discreetly nodded his head that the crowd rose and turned their attention back to the plays. Simon began again.

'Oh! Rise up all ye kings three . . .'

* * *

Bullock still could not believe what Falconer had told him — that a murder had taken place in the town and he had not known of it. What Falconer had learned from Jehozadok was that the body of old Solomon had been ignored by all who passed it. He had been left in a crumpled heap like so many rags until one of his own race had happened down the lane where he had met his fate. No doubt the Christians who had walked by would claim if questioned that they thought he was merely drunk. But still Bullock could not stomach their callousness towards another human soul, Jew or not. The body had already been whisked away, and buried according to the rituals practised by the Jews. It did begin to explain the fracas at Petysance's procession, and the young Jew's threat. He just hoped another life would not be lost in some vengeful act. But, with the body gone and the inward-looking Jews closing ranks, there seemed little he could do about the death, except keep his ear to the ground.

As for Falconer, he was curious about Solomon's conversation with Jehozadok before his death. Was there a clue in what he had said? Were his death and the 'accidental' death of the monk linked in any way? After all, Solomon had been in the courtyard of St Frideswide's on the day of Brother Adam's untimely death. There was so much information and as yet so little sense to it all. But first Falconer had his duty to his friend Bacon to perform, knowing that amongst the other prisoners released by 'Lord' Thomas would have been Zerach de Alemmania. The secret letter from Friar Bacon suddenly burned hot in the pouch at his waist. It was not only that he wished to deliver it as soon as possible, but he also wanted to know its contents himself. He resolved to find a way to persuade Zerach to open it in his presence. He muttered an apology to Bullock and followed a few other souls who were drifting away from the plays. Casting a glance back as he walked under the arch into Fish Street, he saw the troubadour Robert Kemp stride on stage in the role of Herod and threaten to kill the kings and the new-born babe.

The heavy greyness of the sky was ushering in the gloom of evening rapidly and Falconer folded his arms across his chest to protect himself from the cold. The market was gone from the street, but jugglers, puppeteers and dancing bear trainers still entertained the ebb and flow of people by the light of flickering torches. Deep shadows hung over the corners furthest from the flames, and Falconer kept a weather eye open for the nightwalkers who would soon be emerging to rob the unwary. The lane down to Zerach's house was deep in gloom, and Falconer did not relish standing too long exposed to the silence that hung over it. Everyone it seemed was at the plays.

His urgent knocking on the door only elicited a tremulous voice from the other side of the oak after some considerable time.

'Who's there?'

'My name is Falconer. I am a regent master at the university and a friend of Roger Bacon.'

'I do not know you or him.'

Falconer hesitated. Was this the wrong man after all? No — the clues fitted his name too well. The play on the meaning of his second name — Germany in the French tongue — and the initial letters of his names — Z and A, Omega and Alpha — confirmed it. Surely the man was just frightened, as anyone had a right to be who had been incarcerated by the King and threatened with the scaffold. He needed to convince Zerach de Alemmania that he was truly who he said he was.

'Roger had a thesis — *possunt fieri instrumenta volandi.* Surely he told you of that?'

The voice sounded unconvinced. 'He told many people of the possibility of making a flying machine.'

'Yes, but he only told a few close friends and colleagues that someone was attempting to make it reality.'

Falconer prayed that Zerach had been close enough to the friar to be let in on this secret. There came the sound of a bolt being pulled back, and a pale, drawn face was pressed to the narrow gap as the door was opened. There was a question on the man's lips, and Falconer grinned in embarrassment.

'Yes, I am the fool who took Roger at his word.'

'Come in, quickly.'

Zerach grabbed Falconer's arm and drew him through the half-open door, slamming it securely behind him. With a trembling hand, he threw the bolt back into place, only then relaxing and allowing himself a tentative smile. He ushered Falconer into the large room where the regent master had seen all Zerach's texts and bade him sit where he could. Falconer moved a pile of books from a chair and sat down. The Jew remained standing, pacing back and forth in front of the dead ashes in the grate. It was as if he was in conflict with himself — fearful of what might have happened to him, yet full of anger at the ones who had put him in that predicament. Falconer could not blame him and sought to calm the man with inconsequential conversation on the nature of his experiments with flying devices. At present he had to admit they were no more than a child's toys, that could glide to earth if projected from one of the towers that dotted the city walls. Eventually Zerach was sufficiently in control of himself to enquire why Falconer had called.

Falconer rose and drew a stiff package from the folds of his robe. He offered it to Zerach. 'This is from our mutual friend.'

'Bacon?' Zerach hesitated, then eagerly grasped the package and broke the seal on its outer surface. He stood transfixed and read the spidery scrawl that filled the surface of the paper. A frown clouded his features.

'What has he to say?' asked Falconer gently.

'Oh. He commends the bearer of this letter to me — but then is anxious that I no longer waste my time on what he calls speculative alchemy. No matter that I have spent every year since he was bundled off to France in seeking the quintessence at his instigation.'

Zerach sounded a little peevish. But Falconer knew the speed at which Roger Bacon's mind moved on from one concept to another, far outstripping the mortals who surrounded him. It was perfectly normal for him to be denigrating that which he was most interested in but a few years earlier as his understanding of the universe grew. Zerach read on.

'He suggests I investigate so-called practical alchemy, and maintains he has blended a pure metal, for which he has no name, with iron and produced a plate of unusual hardness which could be used for armour. He also supplies a recipe for a black powder that explodes when set afire and bids me replicate his trials. Hmm . . .'

Falconer saw the spark of excitement ignite in Zerach's eyes. He had soon overcome his annoyance at Bacon's initial comments and was obviously eager to try these new experiments for himself. For the moment, thoughts of those who had denounced him, and the face from the past he had seen the day the actors arrived, were suppressed in Zerach's zeal to pursue his scientific goals.

Glad to have carried out the friar's wishes and learned something of the contents of the letter, Falconer was content to leave the man to his science. Promising to return and hear how he progressed, he took his leave of the distracted alchemist and returned to the chill of Pennyfarthing Street. Although all he desired now was to return to the warmth of

Aristotle's Hall, he could not put the bungled attempt on de Askeles's life out of his mind. Nor the associated death, as he saw it, of Solomon the Jew. Indeed, he could now concentrate solely on them, and even though he was convinced the murderer of the monk was still at large in the form of Ralph the carpenter, he decided it would do no harm to observe the actions of the troupe of players. He therefore made his way back to the courtyard of St Frideswide's Church.

* * *

Will Plome had lighted the torches that were strategically placed around the stage. The scenes would carry on late into the evening, and de Askeles wanted to ensure that every gesture was visible to the crowd, and the King and nobles who watched from the Prior's raised dais. Though he would not admit it, Stefano was nervous. As Robert Kemp, playing Herod, questioned the three kings about the baby Jesus, he peered out from the side of the stage at where the King of England sat. Henry's grey head and forked beard stood out from those who surrounded him. The lights around the stage cast deep shadows in the wells of his eye sockets, making his gaunt face even more starkly lined. So old and yet so powerful. De Askeles wondered if his son, Edward, ever chafed to be King and dreamed of regicide to remove this ancient impediment from his path. He knew what he would do in the same circumstances. In the meantime, it was this old man he would seek to impress in order to wheedle his way to the riches he so eagerly craved. Scanning the crowd, he spotted Petysance the priest in the front row of those standing in the yard. He took another swig from the flagon of wine at his side.

The ill-shapen form of the shaven headed Will Plome lumbered up the steps at the side of the stage, and went to poke his fingers through the bars of the cage that held the green monkey. The creature chittered happily at the attention it was receiving and pressed its black furry head against the bars, allowing Will to scratch it. A malicious thought crossed the drink-fogged mind of de Askeles, and he moved to where Will stood. Dressed as the Devil in long black robes, with the great horned mask held under one arm like a second head, de Askeles was a commanding figure. He leaned over Will and hissed in his ear. 'Give the monkey to me.'

Will looked fearfully into de Askeles's glittering eyes. He knew the man hated the attention he paid Ham and thought him capable of any evil. The fact he was dressed as the Devil only seemed to confirm that feeling. But why should he want Ham now? The worry that twisted his ugly features urged de Askeles on.

'The monkey — give it to me now.'

'Why?' Will was sure he didn't want to know the answer but could not stop himself asking. De Askeles laughed.

'Because the next scene is the Slaying of the Innocents, and I am tired of sticking a knife into a rag doll only to have it sewn together again for the next time. This time the monkey shall be the innocent, and we shall see some real blood.'

Will Plome's squeal of distress was cut across by a woman's harsh voice.

'Stop that.'

Agnes Cheke strode out of the darkness and put herself between Will and his tormentor. She pulled the distraught fool to her bosom like some grotesque, oversized baby, muffling his cries in the ample folds of her dress. De Askeles raised his fist to hit her but was stopped by an urgently hissed whisper from the edge of the stage. It was Simon Godrich, dressed as one of the women who was due to have her innocent babe slain.

'Stefano, you should be on stage now.'

De Askeles lowered his arm. 'You two are a fine pairing. I will have you as a side-show — the Ugliest Woman in the World and her overgrown babe.'

With that he crammed the Devil mask on his head and strode off to make his appearance through the trapdoor, having blown the glowing embers of vengeance in Agnes's and Will's souls into a raging fire.

* * *

'I now see fiends in great swarms
From Hell coming for me.
I have done so much harm,
I now see coming my great foe,
To fetch me off to Hell.
I bequeath here in this place
My soul to be with Satanas.
I die, I die, alas, alas!
Here I may no longer dwell.'

Herod, with his pointed Saracen's beard, fell to the ground as the form of the Devil rose out of the trapdoor with smoke issuing around him. De Askeles raised his arms and masked off the figure of Herod from the audience milling in the courtyard. Spontaneous cheers arose as the Devil descended and the smoke cleared revealing an empty stage — Herod had been transported to hell.

'Come,' whispered Falconer, and he took Peter Bullock by the arm, drawing him to the edge of the crowd. The constable protested.

'But the plays haven't ended yet.'

'I am not leaving. But I am curious as to how the effects are achieved. We will see more of the artifice from the side of the stage.'

Bullock grumbled that he did not wish to see how things worked — it would only spoil the magic. But Falconer persisted and the constable followed him to the right side of the stage, where the regent master peered with curiosity underneath the staging. He was rewarded with the sight of de Askeles and Robert Kemp making their way in the constricted space to the opposite side of the stage. There, squatting on her haunches, was the plump figure of Agnes Cheke, holding a candle to guide the actors out of the maze of timbers. Above their heads the Betrayal of Christ had begun with the mellifluous tones of Simon Godrich reciting Jesus's words at the Last Supper.

'For now you see the time has come,
When signs and shadows all are done.
A great sacrifice begin I shall,
To save mankind from his sins all.'

The constable followed the unfolding of the Betrayal with rapt attention, but Falconer's gaze was drawn to a figure at the edge of the stage. He poked around in his pouch and drew out his eye-lenses to see the figure better. It was John Peper and he was beckoning to someone in the audience, but it was impossible for Falconer to distinguish who it was in the sea of faces. He bent down to peer under the stage in case this afforded him a better view. The candle, left by Agnes just beneath the stage, lit this nether world better than that of the upper. But it only afforded him the sight of a curious moving tableau of bodies cut off at the waist, making him guess at the identity of those who passed before his eyes.

First he saw the plain linen skirt of a woman, probably Agnes, as he knew she was on that side of the stage. Nevertheless, in his frustration he realized it could equally have been Margaret, or even one of the men playing the part of a woman. Whoever it was moved to the back of the stage. He decided on Agnes until something told him otherwise. Then two other figures came from the direction of the crowd. One wore plain hose and his legs were stocky. Will Plome. The other wore a black robe that fell to the ground and almost hid the soft leather boots on his feet. The robe could have belonged to monk, priest or Jew, or even one of the actors dressed ecclesiastically to represent an angel. The two men paused at the steps to the far side of the stage.

Straightening, Falconer twisted the metal frame of his eye-lenses as he strained to make out the two figures, but they were hidden in darkness. On stage, de Askeles, now acting the role of Peter, swung a sword and appeared to cut off the ear of one of the amateur actors playing the part of Malchus. The crowd gasped as Simon Godrich in the role of Jesus bent down and picked up the 'ear' from the stage and restored it to the unfortunate Malchus's head. From his vantage point, Falconer could see Simon palm the fake ear as he rubbed the side of the actor's head and transfer it to a pocket in his robes. Stooping, he returned to his half-world. The legs of Will Plome had gone, and the other man paced back and forth in the tiny area off stage. His pacing stopped as someone came down the steps from the stage, and both men stood facing each other, toe to toe. For a while they stood motionless, then one stamped his leather-clad foot and turned his back.

Falconer stood up and grabbed Bullock's arm.

'Who was it left the stage last?'

'Judas. Why do you want to know?'

Falconer was exasperated by the constable's obtuseness.

'Yes, but who played that part?'

'John Peper,' replied Bullock, puzzled.

Falconer quickly rehearsed in his mind what he knew of everyone's position around the stage. Agnes (or was it Margaret?) was at the back of the stage. Will too had gone in that direction. Someone had come out of the audience and spoken to John Peper. But who was it, and why did Peper call him forth?

At that moment the scene ended and actors rushed hither and thither, the more amateur ones falling over each other in their rush to dress for the next scene. Some even returned to their friends in the courtyard, their part in the plays over. When Falconer's view of the stage side was next clear, both John Peper and the other man were lost in the mêlée. The stranger could be back in the crowd and the actor anywhere.

Several of the performers were now wearing black gowns on which were tablet-shapes of yellow cloth. This was the garb the law demanded the Jews of England wore to identify them to the Christian community they lived within. Wearing grotesque parodies of the Jewish elders' long beards, the actors pushed Simon Godrich to that part of the stage that was set up as Pilate's palace. The crowd booed and hissed as the fake Jews acted out their part in Christ's Passion. Falconer just hoped this enactment would not revive the anger of those who had witnessed the young hotheads defiling the cross earlier in the day. He still anxiously scanned the other side of the stage area through his lenses.

For a moment he could not see de Askeles anywhere — he certainly was not on stage. Then he saw a shaft of torchlight playing on a head of long blond hair at the side of the stage. De Askeles stood alone with the white and gilded robe of God in his left hand, his head tilted back and his right hand holding something to his lips. He obviously was not in the present scene, and was making ready for the Ascension scene that must follow. Falconer had no doubt that de Askeles would be playing God.

Just then, a shadow seemed to free itself from the deep gloom on the far side of the stage, and Falconer thought be saw de Askeles turn sharply round. Next the actor was tumbling down the steps that led down off stage. Ducking down, Falconer was in time to see a booted foot kick over the candle that had stood there, plunging the understage into darkness.

'Hey! Where are you going?' shouted a startled Bullock, as a resolute Falconer dived under the stage and, bent low, scuttled beneath the performers' feet as they began enacting the Resurrection and Ascension.

CHAPTER FOURTEEN

LUCIFER: Some of my charge shall it be
To make mankind all to do amiss.
Ruffian, my friend, fair and free,
Look that you keep man from bliss.

The Fall of Lucifer

Reaching the other side of the stage with nothing worse than a sharp crack to the head as he emerged, Falconer peered around in the gloom. He fully expected to see a body, and maybe the retreating figure of Ralph the carpenter, having carried out the murder he had bungled days earlier. But there was nothing save a pile of discarded clothes on top of a large chest. He rummaged through the robes, thinking to uncover the body of Stefano de Askeles. He uncovered nothing save the smell of sweat.

'What are you doing back here? You're not one of the performers.'

Agnes Cheke, her face flushed, bustled out of the darkness and began to tidy the robes that Falconer had tossed about in his fruitless search. As she stacked them in a neat pile, she peered at him through the gloom.

'You're that nosy master who was with the constable. Always prying and asking questions. Well, there's nothing for you to find. You shouldn't even be here.'

But she did not make him leave, merely scurried around tidying up like a mother hen, with half an ear to what was occurring on the stage. Suddenly she started, paying more attention to the words being uttered by Simon Godrich, and mumbling along with the actor.

> *'My drops of blood I will present*
> *To my Father with all good intent . . .'*

Then she craned her neck to see behind the backcloth and gasped. 'He's not there.'

'Who?' asked Falconer, curious.

'Stefano. He is supposed to be God, and in a few moments Jesus — Simon — ascends the ladder into his arms. Stefano should be on that upper platform already.'

Falconer followed Agnes's gaze, just discerning a raised platform reached by a ladder behind the backcloth. He felt sure now that de Askeles was in no fit state to carry out his role and wondered what the King and the rest of the people crowded into the courtyard would think of the absence of God. At that very moment, the imposing form of de Askeles, clad in gilded robes and with the mask of God firmly fixed upon his head, appeared from the gloom at the back of the stage. With no more than a grunt to acknowledge their presence he scuttled up the ladder.

Agnes breathed a sigh of relief.

'He must have forgotten what came next. He came from where God's throne is set for the Last Judgement. That's what drink does for you.'

Falconer, convinced from over the other side of the stage that the stumbling de Askeles had been stabbed and was dying, had to accept that the man must merely have been drunk. It was possible to assume a murder without a body, but not when the body was walking around and acting. He did notice a strange look in Agnes's eyes, but whether it was shock or puzzlement he could not decide. Then, as quickly as it had come, it was gone, and she returned to tidying the sweaty robes. On stage Simon sang '*Ascendo at Patrem Meum*', then fell into the arms of God.

* * *

Henry bowed his head and mumbled a quiet prayer to himself at the sight of the face of God towering over the group of actors on the stage. King of England he might be, but he was also a devout man, who had caused a golden shrine to be made for the bones of St Edward, and had presented a vial of Christ's blood to Westminster Abbey. Around him, Roger Mortimer, Thomas de Cantilupe and the other nobles in his entourage, ever mindful to imitate the actions of their better, also bowed their heads. On the King's throne, Thomas Symon, Lord of Misrule, sat oblivious of the devotions around him. The plays were mesmerizing and he had never had the opportunity to actually see such a presentation. Before coming to Oxford, his life had been restricted to the boundaries of his father's farm. Not even the local lord's manor house had been part of his experience. At Christmastide entertainment had been limited to the rustic humour of a mummers' play. Even the first few years he had spent in Oxford had not provided him with such a spectacle. Now he was witnessing it from the loftiest of viewpoints.

He wriggled in his seat as the plays reached their climax. The night was cold, but the coursing of blood in his body made him feel hot. After Christ's Ascent into Heaven, there only remained to depict the overcoming of Antichrist and the Last Judgement. He waited impatiently through the interminable pause as the stage was set. From inside the church could be heard the voices of the monks intoning '*Quem queritis?*'. The eternal question — whom do you seek in the manger, O shepherds? — hardly penetrated the excited buzz of the common crowd in the courtyard. But suddenly, over this noise, a voice rang out. A priest Thomas immediately recognized as Edward Petysance of St Aldate's Church was emboldened to approach the rostrum on which the King and his court sat.

'Your Majesty, I pray you attend the church of St Aldate's while you are in Oxford. The arm of St Eldad now rests in this church, and has already witnessed miracles.'

Petysance's voice cut across the other conversations in the courtyard, and most of those closest to the King turned to stare at his presumption. It was not normal to pester royalty so, and those who heard Petysance thought the priest must have taken leave of his senses. Perhaps the possession of the holy relic had turned his mind. The King, startled by the interruption, merely waved his hand noncommittally at the priest and leaned across to speak to de Cantilupe. Thomas Symon could not make out what he said and was about to command the former Chancellor to explain when the plays recommenced. The Lord of Misrule returned his gaze to the stage, noticing as he did so that his master, William Falconer, was standing at the stage side looking somewhat downcast. He hoped that the master had heard that his stratagem had worked and that the prisoners had been released. He would take great pleasure in cheering Falconer up if he had not — and what a story he had to tell besides of his time as 'King of England'.

As Petysance melted back into the crowd, seemingly unconcerned by his rebuff, all eyes turned back to the actors. The defeat of the Antichrist by the Archangel Michael was performed to the left of the long stage, where Hell stood. John Peper was acting the role of the Archangel, and he spoke the words as though he had something else on his mind. However, he wielded the sword with venom, and the Antichrist, in the form of Robert Kemp, seemed glad to fall back into the yawning hole of the trapdoor, which was left open as a dire warning to the sinners in the crowd.

A curtain was drawn back at the extreme right of the stage, where now stood the Mansions of Heaven. The backcloth before the crowd's admiring eyes held depictions of blossoming trees of cherry, apple and pear, creating the image of Celestial Paradise. In front of the cloth stood the throne of God with two taut ropes stretched out above it. These were to raise God into the heavens at the end of the scene, and at the other end of the ropes several burly men stood ready to carry out their task. On the throne in a rather stiff posture sat de Askeles, dressed as God with the imposing sunburst mask over his face.

The final scene required Archangel Michael to lead the characters Enoch and Elias from the pit of hell to the throne of God. The actors playing their parts, two silversmiths who the rest of the year toiled in their workshops in the High Street, looked expectantly at John Peper. They were ready to take their lead from him, but he just stood stock still, as though he had forgotten his lines. He tried to begin his speech.

> *'Now to Heaven where the Lord is,*
> *Shall . . .'*

Only the two men on the stage saw clearly the anguish in Peper's eyes, and at first thought he was angry at his own error. But then Peper gave out an inhuman groan that chilled the onlookers' hearts, and lurched across the stage, sword still in his hand. Later, several people said he struck God down in silence, others that he cried something like 'Defiler of women!' All could aver that John Peper drew his sword back, and impaled Stefano de Askeles on the throne of God with a single blow.

CHAPTER FIFTEEN

LUCIFER: Alas! for all our woe and wickedness!
I am bound so fast in this plight and cheer,
And never away from hence may pass
But lie in Hell with all for ever still.

The Fall of Lucifer

The rest of the night was pandemonium. The crowd gasped as one, and those nearest the stage instinctively pushed backwards to escape. Knots of onlookers collapsed in heaps, and the courtyard suddenly became a maelstrom of tangled limbs. Those still on their feet fled for the nearest exit, not caring whom they flattened in the process. The men-at-arms in front of the King sprang up and surrounded him, ensuring that the homicide did not become a regicide. In the process, Thomas Symon was unceremoniously tumbled from his throne, and ended up sitting on the hard wooden platform entangled in the oversize cloak he had borrowed from the King.

Peter Bullock was the first to regain his composure, and yelled at the two startled silversmiths on stage to take hold of John Peper. They took one look at the frenzied actor and, despite the fact that he was still struggling to pull the sword from the corpse, fled to safety down the steps. As Bullock cursed and tried to heave his crooked bulk on to the stage, Peper gave up his unequal struggle with the transfixed sword and darted across the boards in their wake. Before he reached the steps, however, he spotted Falconer barring his path. The master looked well able to defend himself, and Peper took the only other route out. He dived through the trapdoor and down into Hell.

Falconer and Bullock arrived at the mouth of the trap at the same moment, and peered into the smoke that was still rising from it.

'Let me go first,' said Falconer. 'I am a little more agile than you.'

Bullock grunted, but let his friend drop through the trapdoor first anyway. Then he sat on the edge and fell the few feet to the ground beneath. Falconer was kicking over the brazier of smouldering wood chippings that was causing the smoke, but he could not see Peper anywhere.

'You go that way and I'll go this.' Falconer pointed along the front of the understage and went himself towards the back. Bullock set off in an ungainly crouch. The smoke of hell still hung around under the stage, and the constable began to cough as he drew it into his lungs. He could hear Falconer also wheezing away to his left but could not see him in the darkness. The innumerable struts that held the stage up turned the area into a maze, and Bullock felt disorientated. He imagined he could walk past Peper crouching in the dark only feet away from him and be none the wiser. Gradually his eyes did adjust a little, and he could make out a large barrel lying on its side ahead of him. He approached it with care and peered in the open end. Peper was not in hiding in it — it was half full of stones. Bullock wondered what it was doing here, then realized how the sound of the earthquake in the Crucifixion scene had been effected. He had almost reached the end of the stage and the weak shaft of light that penetrated the gloom there, when he heard Falconer calling away to his right. His voice was muffled and strange, almost disembodied. Bullock shuddered but moved in the direction from which he thought the voice had come. When he found him, Falconer was fingering the heavy cloth that blanked the back of the understage off from the lane that ran beside the church. It had been roughly torn away at one corner and, though it was as dark outside as underneath the stage, it was clear their quarry was gone.

They made their way back to the trapdoor and stuck their heads up into the dying light of the torches that surrounded the stage. Most of the crowd had gone, except for those for whom the sight of death was an attraction. They were the sort who would have derived bloodthirsty satisfaction from seeing the Oxford merchants whom Falconer had freed dancing on the end of a rope. Better still if they had been drawn and quartered. Falconer was glad he had deprived them of that pleasure. The King and his entourage were long gone, the men-at-arms no doubt having broken a few heads in the crowd to ensure a speedy and safe escape for the monarch. Only a forlorn Thomas Symon sat on the edge of the King's platform, stripped of his purple robe and his title. A huddle of figures, including two actors still dressed as angels, hovered around the slumped body, which was still impaled on the murder weapon.

Falconer used his powerful arms to push himself on to the edge of the trap, and bent down to offer assistance to Peter Bullock.

'I think I will come out at the front of the stage, if you don't mind. I am no saltatore.'

Falconer acknowledged the constable's caution, got to his feet and went over to the body of de Askeles. By the time Bullock had emerged from the front of the stage, and climbed the steps at one side, Falconer was already assisting in the removal of the sword, and the mask from the actor's head. It was almost a relief when the corn-coloured locks of de Askeles fell out of the mask — at least it was not another murder by mistaken identity. His face was a waxy colour and the eyes closed — he seemed almost peaceful. Quite unlike the man in life. As they laid him down on the stage, one arm slumped away from those holding him and slapped down on the wooden floor. The thud alarmed those supporting de Askeles and they almost dropped him. Robert Kemp and Simon Godrich went to fetch a hurdle to carry the body away, but Falconer stooped over it, examining the wound.

'At least you can't tell me that the carpenter did this one,' commented the constable. 'I have scores of witnesses to say John Peper killed him — including the King of England himself! And I do not doubt that he was responsible for the earlier attempt that resulted in the monk's death. I should never have listened to you and released him — this would not have happened if I hadn't.'

To Bullock's exasperation, Falconer just ignored him and stared off into space. The constable knew, to his cost usually, that the regent master always had that look when an earth-shattering idea had struck him. Still, he could not see how this death could be anything other than straightforward — everyone had seen Peper land the blow that killed de Askeles. Even William Falconer would have to admit that. Bullock realized he must have spoken his thoughts out loud when Falconer replied, 'What? Of course I do not deny that John Peper thrust a sword into de Askeles. But the question is, did he kill him?'

* * *

The King's hall at Beaumont was once again in a flurry of activity. Henry paced around his rooms, scattering servants before him. Eventually the Queen calmed him down, but he was still resolved to leave Oxford early the following morning. He gave the order for a return to London and sent for Thomas de Cantilupe. The fearful ex-Chancellor entered the King's chamber thinking that once again his world had toppled around him. And inevitably he blamed Regent Master Falconer for the whole misfortune. If it was not the Lord of Misrule fiasco that had angered the King, then murder before his very eyes had. And it was all Falconer's fault — he seemed to attract death to him like lightning to the loftiest tree. A pity that he had not been blasted into oblivion like the tree.

The King beckoned de Cantilupe to him peevishly, looking all of his considerable years. His face was lined with age, and if de Cantilupe had not known his drooping eyelid was a family trait, he might have supposed Henry suffered from the half-dead disease. However, the King clearly had full control over both his arms, which he waved in agitation.

'The world is turned upside down without the need for a Lord of Misrule, de Cantilupe.'

Thomas started to apologize for the stupid idea, but Henry cut him off.

'What with de Montfort's sons and Berkeley and Bassett marauding in the countryside around the marshes of Ely, robbers who do not even respect the dignity of the King, and now this murder, it's clear we need some discipline in our realm.'

'Your Majesty, I could not agree more.'

De Cantilupe would grovel as far as necessary to preserve his newly won position. Let the Devil take William Falconer — he would never listen to him again. The King thrust a parchment and quill into his hands.

'Take this down.'

De Cantilupe gasped — the King was trying his new resolve by asking him to take notes. But if Henry wanted him as a scribe then one he would be. He crossed to a table where stood an inkwell, and spread the parchment before him. The King resumed his pacing as he spoke.

'Item: that watches be renewed in all townships, which have been allowed to lapse, and by honest and able men. Item: that the hue and cry be followed according to ancient custom . . . Where was the hue and cry this night, I would like to know? Don't write that down . . . Write this: All who refuse and neglect to follow a hue and cry shall be taken into custody as aiders of the wrongdoers. Item: let four or six men according to the size of the township be chosen to follow the hue and cry swiftly . . . and with bow and arrow or other light arms to be provided at the cost of the township. Let me see . . . Item: that no stranger abide in the township except by day, and that he depart while it is still light. Item: that the bailiffs and burghers of all townships be ordered that if any passing merchant show them money he is carrying, then they must ensure his safe conduct through the township. And if he loses aught then let him be indemnified by the said burghers. There, that will do. I have a mind to clear all the highways between market towns of any undergrowth also, but that will suffice for now.'

De Cantilupe nodded at the sagacity of the King and prayed that the murdering troubadour would be found soon and given his just deserts.

* * *

It was the middle of the night, and freezing cold, but Falconer seemed to be able to ignore this discomfort. He was far more interested in the body of Stefano de Askeles, which now lay before him. He had persuaded Peter Bullock to arrange to bring it to Aristotle's Hall, where it had been laid out on the long communal table the students used for their meals. He had had to clear the crumbs, wine dregs and other debris of the last meal before the body could be placed there. Falconer had irreligious thoughts of the Last Supper and the body and blood of Christ as he surveyed de Askeles's mortal remains. Then he shook his head to clear it and pondered his task. First he doused the embers that still glowed in the fireplace to prevent the warmth from disturbing the study he intended to make of the body.

He slowly began to undress de Askeles, which proved awkward as the death rigor was now setting in. Underneath the white gown with gilded edges was another, more bloodied robe, which he proceeded to remove also. Eventually all the clothing was discarded, and the corpse was revealed as yellow as the candles that lit the scene. Falconer seemed oblivious of the group of staring faces at the top of the staircase that led to the students' sleeping quarters. The delivery of a body was not something that could be carried out quietly, and the students had been roused from their slumbers. Now they stared at an unbelievable sight, used as they were to their master's strange pursuits. On the very table where they had imagined their imminent Christmas feast lay a naked corpse that Falconer was poking and prodding as though in search of some hidden meaning. Falconer barely halted his examination to let the students know he was indeed aware of their existence.

'I ask no more than that you keep out of the way . . . and learn.'

The door leading out on to the lane opened, and Bullock appeared with a grey, nondescript man with a bald patch that resembled a monk's tonsure, and he carried a bundle held tightly under his arm. Falconer strode over to him.

'Ah, Bonham. Thank you for coming at such an ungodly hour. I need your expertise.'

Richard Bonham was also a regent master at the university, lecturing normally in rhetoric. He was a number of years younger than Falconer, but his bald head and serious demeanour gave the impression of a much older man. Falconer often disagreed with his views but respected him for his obsessive interest in a particular area of knowledge that had to be kept a deadly secret. Successive popes had expressly forbidden the anatomizing of the human body, and few people were bold enough to contravene the papal interdictions. A handful of scholars quietly boasted of having explored one or two corpses in a lifetime of study. Falconer knew Richard Bonham had dissected at least four in as many years.

In response to Falconer's statement, Bonham looked first greedily at the body, then fearfully at the ring of students above him.

'I cannot do that. Here. With everyone looking on.'

He turned to leave, but Falconer stayed him with a hand on his arm. 'They are all thirsters after knowledge, like you and me. Besides, I am not certain we will need your . . . implements.'

Falconer pointed at the neatly tied leather bundle that Bonham clutched in his nervous hands. He knew it contained a set of fearsomely sharp knives which Bonham used to cut precisely into the flesh and muscle of the bodies he dissected. Falconer had seen one flayed and laid out like meat in a butcher's shop in the man's basement. His own curiosity had overcome the horror of seeing the innermost parts of a human being revealed in such a fashion. Others might not view it so impartially and scientifically. Bonham and his like had to be very cautious. Falconer continued, 'A superficial examination may be enough.'

Thus reassured, the little master returned his gaze to the body on the table. Crossing the room to it, he ran his delicate hands over the corpse's limbs, then over the eyes.

'Hmm. The facial muscles are stiffening, but the extremities not so much. So he has been dead a short time. Perhaps the length of time between sext and nones. Yet not quite as cold as the air, so he died less than half a day ago.'

Bullock began to protest. 'What is all this about, William? We know exactly when he died — we were all there. And we saw who killed him. Even you have to admit it was John Peper.'

'Patience, Peter,' said Falconer. 'You may think you do not need to know what Master Bonham can tell you, but please at least indulge my whim for a little while.'

Bullock blew his breath out in exasperation. It emerged as a visible plume in the coldness of the room. Unaware of the exchange, Bonham had continued to examine the corpse.

'Note the typical waxiness of the skin.' He paused as he poked his fingers in the gash in the lower chest where John Peper had plunged the sword. 'I presume you closed his eyes and washed the body.'

Falconer shook his head, and Bonham look puzzled.

'Then where is all the blood? Show me his clothes.'

'Here they are.' Falconer went over to where he had dropped the two layers of clothes and offered Bonham the white gown first. There was hardly a drop of blood around the tear made by the sword. Though there were stains on the hem, which was held in crumpled folds by the dried blood. But when they examined the robe de Askeles had worn underneath, they found it covered in blood. Bonham turned the second robe over and over in his hands. Suddenly he threw it down and rushed back to the body, struggling with its bulk.

'Help me turn it over,' he said impatiently.

Falconer stepped forward and together they rolled over de Askeles's body. Excitedly, Falconer pointed at the marking on the buttocks. 'What are these bruises doing here?'

Bonham smiled. 'They are not bruises. You see, when we are alive our blood is spread evenly around our body. On death it falls to the lowest points in the body. That bruising is simply congestion of blood at those points.'

'Strange, is it not, that it does not then show up so much on his back? He has been lying flat all the time since his death.'

Bonham acknowledged Falconer's comments and was about to respond when he spotted something else. 'Look at this. That's what I was looking for.'

Falconer peered closely where the little anatomist was pointing. There were two wounds in the flesh of the actor's back, not one. He lifted the body up on its side, and looked first at de Askeles's back, then at his chest. He pointed to the higher wound in the back.

'This cut aligns with the gash in his chest. And that fits with the fact that John Peper was below de Askeles when he impaled him on the sword.'

Bullock could not resist interrupting. 'Ah. You do admit Peper was on the end of the sword. Not some demon.'

Falconer ignored him, and continued, pointing to the lower wound, 'While this one is smaller and bloodier.'

'Exactly,' shouted Bonham in triumph, as though Falconer were a slow student who had suddenly been led through a logical thesis to a full understanding of the concept under debate. 'If you look at the second garment you showed me, the blood is all on the back, not the front. Meaning . . .'

He paused to allow his 'student' to draw the inevitable conclusion. Falconer obliged. 'That de Askeles was first stabbed in the back.'

Bullock was still puzzled. 'But the blow from John Peper? Could it not have caused both wounds?'

Falconer and Bonham looked knowingly at each other, but it was Falconer who spoke first. 'Unlikely. The sword went straight through him and stuck into the throne and I drew it out cleanly myself — it could not have pierced his back again. We are left with the inevitable conclusion that de Askeles was killed twice.'

CHAPTER SIXTEEN

GOD: Ay! wicked pride shall ever work thee woe
My joy thou hast made amiss.
I may well suffer: my will is not so
That they should part thus from my bliss.

The Fall of Lucifer

'Thank you for your expert opinion, master. Though there were some curiosities about the body that caused me to call for you, I am not sure I would have spotted the other wound myself.'

Falconer led Bonham away from the body on the table towards the door, picking up the tallow lamp that the little regent master had used to light his way through the warren of Oxford streets. It was pitch dark outside and Bonham shivered in the cold as he took his leave. He hesitated in the doorway, as though something were on his mind. Looking over his shoulder at the corpse, he took a deep breath and resolved to say what it was.

'This is the troubadour de Askeles, is it not?'

'That's correct.'

'I cannot be entirely sure — it has been a number of years — but I am more or less certain . . .' He hesitated, and Falconer urged him to continue — he had a feeling the grey man had something important to say. Bonham went on, 'And in death the face takes on a mask-like quality that does not aid recognition . . .'

Falconer's piercing blue eyes bored into Master Bonham as though trying to drag the information out of the man more quickly than he was prepared to give it. 'But . . . ?'

'The man lying on your table there was not called Stefano de Askeles when I saw him last. It was the time of the earthquake in London. The time the King's uterine brothers arrived in England, and he appointed the accursed Aethelmar Archbishop over all the English prelates he could have chosen. What an uproar that caused — I remember there was a parliament at the time and . . .'

Falconer interrupted the flow. 'So, you're talking of some twenty years ago.' He looked at the body. 'He would have been the age my students are now.'

Bonham lowered his voice at the reminder that several young minds, incapable of keeping any secret, might possibly be listening. 'Exactly. It was during my studentship that I met him.'

'What was he doing in Oxford then?'

'The same as all of us.'

'He was a student?' Falconer was surprised.

'And for a while a very good one, until the appeal of the tavern distracted him. And the attractions of a certain type of woman.' Bonham pulled a disapproving face at his last words. The grey man was notorious for his disapproval of any master's indulgence in carnal pleasures. Falconer was not sure Bonham knew of his own peccadilloes in that sphere and had been trying to make a point. The man's face was its usual impenetrable self. Falconer knew as everyone did that masters of the university could not marry, but no one expected them to be celibate. Except Bonham.

'And his name was not de Askeles then. He was plain Stephen Askey from Banbury.'

'Why did he leave?'

'Of his own choice — he grew too lazy to apply himself and a travelling life appealed to him more. I am not surprised to see him return as a troubadour — the life would have suited his erratic nature. Nor am I surprised to see him come to this end. There were many then who would have liked to see him dead. I recall there was one particular occasion when he became ill — it was probably the pox — and he consulted a doctor. The man cured him and was rewarded by Askey's refusal to pay. Indeed, he accused the man of necromancy. Some murderous threat was made by the physician, I believe.'

'Do you recall who the doctor was?'

'One of the Jews, I think. Zeno? Zero? No. Zerach, Zerach de Alemmania was his name.'

* * *

Deulegard was angered by the summons to the presence of Rabbi Jehozadok. The old man might be revered by others in his community, but to the youth he was just what he seemed — a feeble ancient no longer capable of defending his people against the Christian Jew-haters they were forced to live amongst. He pushed his way through the traders on Fish Street, lucky that the previous day's spectacular murder occupied their minds and their tongues. At another time he would have been jostled in return, or worse, for his disrespectful actions. Now the fish merchants stood in huddles with the woodsellers, the silversmiths with the tailors, and speculated on where the murdering actor, John Peper, had gone to ground.

The young Jew went into the Scola, closing the door and blanking off the noise of the market behind him. He climbed the stairs to Jehozadok's private quarters, and swung the door open ready to complain about his peremptory summons. The four people in the room — three men and a youth — surprised him and prevented any initial outburst. They were an ill-matched bunch. Of course Jehozadok himself was there, sitting by the blazing fire but still wrapped in a woollen shawl as though the flames could do nothing to drive the chill of the English winter from his bones. The youth standing at his shoulder was Cressant, and at least he had the grace to be embarrassed at Deulegard's arrival, casting his eyes to the floor. He might have expected Cressant to be there — the spotty youth always questioned the wisdom of every decision Deulegard made for his group. It was not surprising that he should be the traitor on this occasion. But Deulegard was surprised to see the doctor, Zerach de Alemmania. He was a scrawny, cadaverous man whom Deulegard had never had anything to do with. The man kept himself to himself, rarely venturing from his house in Pennyfarthing Street. It was said he consorted with the Devil in his cellar, though he, Deulegard, was not stupid enough to believe such scandal-mongering. He had no idea why Zerach was present, if the matter was to do with the recent furore over the Christians' cross. The presence of the last man was an even greater surprise.

He knew William Falconer was a friend of Jehozadok's, although you could never wholly trust any Christian. When it came to lines being drawn, he was sure he knew where the regent master would stand. And it was not with the other people in this room. The hothead impatiently enquired of Jehozadok what this was all about. 'And why do we have to have this Christian present?'

Jehozadok smiled indulgently, his milky eyes impenetrable. 'This Christian is present because it was he who asked me to gather everyone here together. You should address your questions to him.'

Deulegard spluttered in anger that the foolish old man should be so fawning and subservient to the Christian as to do his bidding in this way. He turned to leave, and was casually thrust back by the rock-like fist of the Christian as though he were of no weight at all. He preserved his young dignity by casting his eyes to the heavens as if to intimate he would humour the foolishness of age and crossed the room to slump in a vacant chair opposite Jehozadok.

'Thank you for your courteous acquiescence.'

Falconer's wry tone did not abash Deulegard, who indicated by a wave of his hands that Falconer could ask all the questions he liked of him. He clearly was not going to answer, but Falconer did not give him a chance to be awkward.

'I will come to you later. In the meantime, I want to speak to your friend.' He stepped over to the confused Cressant and placed a friendly arm on his shoulder. 'Tell me, what was the attack on the procession yesterday all about?'

Deulegard could not resist, and surged forward out of the chair before a startled Cressant could speak. 'Revenge. Revenge for the Christian murder of a Jew.'

'In which another Jew got killed.'

'We must be prepared to give our lives to save ourselves.' This last comment was directed at the blushing Cressant, who cowered behind the frail body of Jehozadok. When Falconer indicated he did not wish to ask him any more questions, Deulegard subsided back into his chair. Falconer touched the rabbi on the shoulder.

'Rabbi, as it is the death of Solomon that has stirred this hornets' nest, will you please be so kind as to tell everyone what you told me yesterday.'

'About Solomon's visit to me just before he died?'

Falconer nodded and Jehozadok's mind drifted back to a morning when Solomon had returned from his nightly duty of guarding the Jews' cemetery outside East Gate. The old man had been very agitated about something — agitated enough to come directly to the rabbi rather than seek out his food and rest in the hovel he shared with his sister. Jehozadok had been the first to speak.

'Solomon. What is the matter?'

The man could hardly put two words together coherently, and Jehozadok spent some time calming him before the story came out. The rabbi remembered the rambling tale almost word for word and pictured the old man telling him.

'I was in my hut like always — you know I stay there to make sure the bodies are safe — especially after the monks took that land away from us. You know I had to move thirty bodies then and re-bury them on the other side of the road. Well, this was a few nights ago — just after those actors arrived. I thought I heard a noise in the graveyard and got up to see what it was. There's often noises, but I'm used to foxes and the like. It was nothing like the noise they make, which is a sort of scratching sound like this . . .'

In Jehozadok's mind Solomon once again scraped the talons that were his work-worn fingers across the surface of the oaken table in this very room. Deulegard snorted with impatience at the rabbi's story and Solomon's wraith disappeared from his mind as Jehozadok continued.

'So, he said he knew it wasn't an animal and lit a candle and went to look. And he saw someone.'

Zerach coughed in obvious embarrassment. 'I suppose I had better own up — he must have seen me. You see, I needed saltpetre for an experiment I was to carry out. And the best place to find it in its purest state is a dunghill or a graveyard.'

Falconer smiled conspiratorially at Jehozadok. 'No, it wasn't you, Master Zerach. Tell them, rabbi, who Solomon said he saw.'

'God. He said he saw God come to take someone away.'

* * *

The troupe of actors were unusually downcast, bearing in mind their common dislike of Stefano de Askeles. Bullock would have imagined that his death would have been a source at least of comfort, if not of rejoicing. Instead they were drifting around the empty stage picking up the scattered remnants of costumes and other properties that had been dropped in the mad scramble the previous night. Simon Godrich fingered the splintered back of God's throne, a raw gash of plain bare wood showing through the ruined gilding. The ropes that would have pulled it to the heavens lay in a limp, slack bundle on the stage. Agnes was attempting to roll up the backcloths. She was having difficulty with the one that showed the darkened clouds of the Flood, which kept creasing as she rolled it. In full daylight the painted blossom of the cherry trees in Paradise was wan, and clearly crudely executed. The magic of the previous day had been completely washed away.

Waiting for Falconer to arrive, Bullock observed Robert Kemp trying to raise the spirits of a dejected Margaret Peper. She was sitting on the edge of the stage, her feet kicking idly at the air. Kemp was standing below her in the courtyard, juggling with three wrinkled apples. They flew in the air in bewildering arcs, and he was making them go higher and higher. Suddenly there was an ear-piercing screech and the juggler took his gaze off the apples. They fell to the ground and he cursed. Beside the wagon, from which the screech had come, squatted Will Plome sucking a bloody finger. Next to him the monkey was shaking the bars of its cage in agitation.

'He bit me,' mumbled the fool around the finger that was still stuck in his mouth. Bullock thought bleakly that even the monkey was out of sorts today.

He was about to give up on his friend when Falconer came striding across the courtyard from the direction of Fish Street. His eyes gleamed with excitement, as though great news had recently been imparted to him. But when Bullock raised a questioning bushy eyebrow, Falconer merely grinned irritatingly and thanked him for gathering the actors together.

'But before I speak to them, I just want to look around at that side of the stage.' He pointed to the left, where last night he had thought he might find the body of de Askeles before the very man, alive and kicking, had pushed past him. When they got there, Falconer poked around on the earth floor and peered at the wooden steps that led up to the stage. He seemed disappointed until he looked more closely at the chest that had been on that side of the stage last night. Clear on its top surface and down the front was a smear of red.

'Could you ask Agnes to come over here, please?'

'What is it? Blood?'

Falconer would not say until Bullock brought Agnes over. He pointed at the mark and asked her what she thought it was. Agnes laughed. 'Holy blood.'

In response to Falconer's questioning look, she amplified. 'You see, Stefano had a lucrative sideline in selling holy relics. He claimed he had obtained them at the Roman Curia, where he had been brought up the bastard son of the Pope. He was a fake, and so was the blood. John made it up for him out of red pigment and water. I remember him spilling some down the trunk.'

Bullock expected Falconer to look disappointed, but he merely smiled broadly. He thanked Agnes, and asked Bullock to assemble the other actors in the courtyard. Then he lingered behind to exchange a few more words with Agnes. The constable did not hear their conversation, but clearly something very satisfactory was said, because Falconer virtually skipped across the courtyard in his pleasure. He gathered the actors around him with a sweep of his arm. The constable imagined that Falconer was going to carry out another round of questioning, and was therefore astounded when Falconer invited them all to Aristotle's Hall.

'We will be celebrating Christmas tomorrow, and I want you to help me perform a mummers' play. I am sure you know one well enough.'

With a glance at Margaret, Simon Godrich probably expressed what was on all their minds.

'Stefano usually played the major role. Besides, how can we perform when John is a fugitive?'

'I think I might manage to stand in for . . . shall we say absent performers. And I may have some news of John by then.'

There was a hungry look of interest in Margaret's eyes, but Falconer would say no more. Uncertain, they eventually agreed to carry out his wishes, and promised to give him a copy of the words he would have to speak himself. As they moved off in a group to plan the staging of the play, Bullock grabbed Falconer's arm.

'What did you mean about John Peper? If you know where he is, you must tell me.'

Falconer as ever was being infuriatingly secretive. 'Tomorrow will be soon enough, Peter. In the meantime, I must speak with an unfortunate wife and mother in the hovels outside South Gate.'

CHAPTER SEVENTEEN

GOD: And though they have broken my Commandment
I rue it full sore and sufferingly;
Nevertheless I will have mine intent;
What first I thought shall still come to be.

The Fall of Lucifer

The communal hall at Aristotle's was transformed. It was normally a gloomy, cramped room dominated by the refectory table that filled the centre of the space. The table spoke eloquently of generations of students who had sat at it. Each stain and scratch was the reminder of some careless youth or boisterous exchange of views over a frugal meal. Some marks were the deliberate carvings of boys who wished to perpetuate their presence with a set of initials and a date. Even these wore away over time as later incumbents rubbed and scrubbed the surface clean, until each student's effort at immortality was no more than a series of indistinguishable ridges criss-crossed with later efforts.

This monument of a table, however, had now been moved to one end of the hall, where it appeared to be but a shadow of its former self. It had taken the combined efforts of Falconer and three students to move, and now the youths were spreading fresh rushes on the floor while Falconer admired their efforts. The hall now looked unusually large, and the table resembled in miniature the stage that stood in the courtyard of St Frideswide's Church. So much so, that fleetingly Falconer thought of acting out the mummers' play on its surface, but the low-ceilinged room would not allow that. No, there would be plenty of room to enact the play on the floor — he did not envisage a large audience for it, after all. And there was another purpose to the whole arrangement anyway — a much more serious purpose.

There came a rumbling noise from out in the lane, which to Falconer sounded like a distant peal of thunder. Then the door to the hall burst open and a red-faced Thomas Symon entered pursuing a small barrel that rolled to a stop at Falconer's feet. Placing his foot on the barrel to steady it, the regent master allowed Thomas to catch his breath before remonstrating with him over the damage that such violent activity would have done to the good ale it contained. The youth grumbled that nothing could make Kepeharm's ale any worse than it was, and that they would have done better to buy a good Poitou or Rhenish wine such as he had drunk at the King's court. Falconer grimaced. 'Will we never hear the end of your exploits as King of England? I wish I had never suggested the mad idea.'

Thomas threw his hands up in concession to Falconer's annoyance. 'I promise never to say another word about it.'

Between them they lifted the barrel on to the table, Thomas biting back a comment about finding a servant at court to carry out such a task. He did not think the regent master would appreciate his jest. Sweating from his exertions, the student offered to tap the barrel and test its contents. He skilfully hit the tap home and though the ale seethed out when he drew some off, in protest at its mishandling, the result was sweet and brown. He poured it greedily down his throat, and Falconer suggested that he leave some for the visitors.

'Who is coming?'

Falconer's face was impassive. 'You will have to wait and see.'

* * *

The constable fussed over the folds of his best tunic, buckling on his sword so that it did not damage the material. The only other time he wore this tunic was when he presented his annual report to the burghers who employed him to keep the peace. He somehow felt it was appropriate for this occasion too and extracted it from the bottom of the chest where it lay for the rest of the year. Yet the event he was attending was pretty much a mystery to him. All Peter Bullock knew was that he was invited to watch the presentation of a mummers' play at Aristotle's Hall, and that he was to arrive at nones. He knew that the troubadours formerly led by Stefano de Askeles — or should he now call him Stephen Askey? — would be performing it. And that did not fill him with relish. With their leader murdered, and one of their troupe the murderer, he could not imagine a very festive atmosphere would prevail. What did pique his curiosity was that he knew Regent Master Falconer always had some devious purpose for mounting such staged events. The man had ulterior motives for the most innocent of actions. Bullock had seen it time and again. Nor did he ever vouchsafe a hint of what he planned to the constable, friend or not. Cynically, Bullock thought this was sometimes because Falconer himself did not know in advance what the results of his actions would be. Then he could claim that he knew all along what would happen without fear of contradiction. On the other hand, he had flushed out many a truth, and many a murderer, in this way. Bullock was sure that today's apparently innocent revel was just such an occasion. That was why he wore his best tunic, flattened his unruly grey hair with water, and hurried off to Aristotle's Hall.

Will Plome could not understand why the other troubadours were so glum. Wasn't Stefano out of the way? And everyone had wanted that, all for their own reasons. There was no one now to stand in his way over Ham. He would give him the best food he could buy, not the rotten fruit that Stefano insisted he have. And he would let him loose from his cage more often, though Agnes had told him to take care or the monkey might run away and never come back. He didn't believe Ham would do that — not like John Peper. He still could not work that out, and went over to Margaret.

'Margaret, why did John run away?'

Margaret's big eyes seemed to overflow with tears, and Agnes quickly led Will away from the sobbing woman. Robert and Simon looked up in embarrassment from the pile of costumes they were sorting through, selecting those that would do for the mummers' play. Herod's costume would do for the Saracen knight, of course, and the storyteller often dressed as the Devil. As for St George, any of the soldier's costumes would do, and their weapons . . .

Simon went grimly over to the wagon and reappeared waving two wooden swords.

'We always used to use these before Stefano . . . before we . . .'

He had no need to finish the sentence — everyone knew it had been at de Askeles's insistence they used real blades. And they had been the cause of two deaths now. It was agreed they would use the wooden swords. As for the parts, Agnes could dress up in the Devil's costume, Robert would be the Saracen knight, and Simon St George. The mock fight would take place over Margaret, playing the part of the King of Egypt's daughter. Agnes hoped she would not notice the irony of a death resulting from two men fighting over her. What a pity they could not resurrect Stefano as they did the knight in the mummers' play. Of course the doctor, who carried out the resurrection, was the part they had inevitably given to Master Falconer. Will, as ever, would simply play the Fool.

'Come on. We need to hurry if we are to be there before nones.'

* * *

Zerach de Alemmania could not imagine why Master Falconer wanted him to go round to Aristotle's Hall that afternoon. The invitation had been brought by a breathless youth who hammered at his door like a second visitation from the King's soldiers. He had been surprised when he peered fearfully through the shutters that screened the interior of the house from the lane to see a skinny youth waiting impatiently on his threshold. There was no sign of any soldiery, so Zerach unbolted his door and peeped out of the gap, holding his shoulder against the door to resist any attack. The skinny youth had merely recited a request from Falconer to come to his hall immediately after nones. Having got the Jew's startled confirmation that he would indeed go, the youth thrust a note into his hand and sped off down the lane. The note, which was also from Falconer, puzzled him even more, but it was worded so insistently, calling on their common friendship with Friar Bacon, and asking for complete secrecy, that Zerach hurried down to his cellar to comply with the request.

* * *

Edward Petysance and the Prior of St Frideswide's were embarrassed to meet each other at the head of the lane leading to Aristotle's Hall. Since their acrimonious encounter in Fish Street a few days before, they had studiously avoided each other. Petysance's flaunting of his holy relic outside the very doors of St Frideswide's Church had angered the Prior, and he had secretly exulted at the fracas with the Jews. For his part, Petysance had been delighted that the Prior's funding of the plays cycle had been sullied by the murder of de Askeles. Neither wished to speak to the other now, but the presence of the Prior's porter, bearing a lantern to light the prelate's way, required they publicly acknowledge each other's presence. The Prior spoke first as they proceeded down the gloomy alley.

'Regent Master Falconer sent a message that he had urgent business appertaining to the . . . er . . . incident at the end of the plays. And that I should arrive shortly after nones. Some scrawny youth brought his request and ran away before I could even think of declining. So I thought it best to come and discover what it was all about.'

Petysance's response was equally terse. 'It would seem the same skinny youth delivered the same message to me. Arrive after nones — but it was to do with the outrage perpetrated on me by the Jews. Though I don't know how he proposes to resolve the matter, when such sacrilege has occurred.'

The Prior muttered a formal concurrence with Petysance's sense of anger at the desecration. The formal niceties observed, they proceeded in tense silence side by side towards Falconer's door.

* * *

'I don't know why you could not have got Cressant to do this for you. He seems willing to do your every bidding.'

Deulegard was fuming at being made to assist the ancient Jehozadok to call upon his friend Falconer. In fact he was astonished that the old man wanted to stir out of doors at all, least of all when night was falling. Jehozadok had not left his house for months, and now he wanted to make some mad excursion to some student hostel. No explanation was forthcoming, other than that it was necessary to go, and that Deulegard was his chosen aide. The journey, nothing for a fit young man, was proving an arduous campaign for the old rabbi. He leaned heavily on Deulegard's arm as they negotiated the mud that threatened at each step to rob Jehozadok of his footing. Every so often they stopped to allow the old man to regain his breath, and Deulegard fumed even more at each delay. The rabbi should not be out at such a time; even he should not be out at such a time. But Jehozadok hobbled stubbornly on. What Deulegard didn't know was that the rabbi could have walked much faster, but his friend Falconer had stipulated that they should be the last to arrive, and he wanted to ensure that that was what happened.

* * *

Simon and Robert carried the chest with their costumes and properties out to the back room in Aristotle's Hall. It had been a kitchen, but the pans that remained were dusty and unused, the hearth cold and piled with logs stored for the fire in the main hall. Falconer could not afford to employ a servant, and the students had little inclination to cook for themselves. What meals were eaten in hall were cold and frugal — when the students could afford it they ate in the taverns they frequented in the evenings. It appeared that little thought had yet been given to the cooking of the pig's head for which they had paid. It sat glassy-eyed and forlorn in the coldest corner of the room.

For now, the kitchen space was a quite satisfactory dressing room for the troubadours. With something familiar to concentrate on that took their minds off the last few days, their spirits rose a little and Agnes felt for the first time that the proposed entertainment might pass off well. Will had brought the little monkey with him — the pair were inseparable now — and it clambered over his shoulders, sitting on his bald pate like some Eastern potentate. Even Margaret raised a smile at Ham as she dressed in the long flowing robe with crescent moons stitched on to it that represented her character — the King of Egypt's daughter. Agnes had no doubt that her acrobatic skills would hold the gaze of the men and boys present, even though her limbs were decorously hidden. There was something about the way even the heaviest gown clung to her figure as she twisted and spun that drew lascivious looks. Robert and Simon stood at one end of the room going through the motions of the sword fight they would shortly present. Like good troubadours, it seemed it was possible for them all to put the matters of the everyday world to one side for a short time at least.

Agnes pulled on the thick black robe that her character, the Devil, required. However, this was not the Devil of the mystery plays but a comical Devil belonging to the older, darker traditions of rural life. Agnes had seen such plays performed in her village as a child, and the Devil had never been an object of fear to her. Even his name was different in the mumming play — Beelzibuz. She still wore a mask for the part, but it was not the awesome mask the crowds had seen at St Frideswide's Church, with its enormous horns and sharp teeth. Today she would wear a mask resembling a skull — a timely reminder of death at this low point of the year. She wondered where John Peper was at this moment — whether he felt that he was at the lowest ebb of his life. And what would happen to him, if he were caught. This Master Falconer seemed a very clever man, and if John had not already escaped Oxford, then she thought Falconer was bound to catch him. She pondered again on what Falconer had said to her when they had arrived at the hall. He had asked for a few changes in the text of the play and returned the book they had given him with some scrawled writing in the margins. He also warned her there might be a surprise at the end. When she had asked what that might be, he had merely smiled enigmatically and left the kitchen.

* * *

When Peter Bullock arrived, he marvelled at the rearrangement of the hall, and the drapery of ivy that Thomas Symon had insisted be hung from the roof beams. He recited a half-forgotten adage from his youth.

> *'At Christmas they do use that Bacchus-weed,*
> *Because they mean, then, Bacchus-like to feed.'*

His eyes took in the barrel of ale that stood prominently on the table, and he sighed when Falconer warned him there was serious business to attend to first. But there was a twinkle in his eye when be added that he fully expected something to celebrate later. The constable was about to ask what when someone knocked at the door of the hall. Falconer winked at Bullock and went to receive whoever had arrived. The constable wandered down to where the students, under the guidance of Thomas Symon, were tying a backcloth from the beams above their heads. He recognized the cloth — a depiction of blossoming trees — as the one from the mystery plays that had represented Paradise. Close to, the painting was crude and the surface cracked where the cloth had been rolled and unrolled countless times. The cloth was arranged in such a way that it hid the door through to the kitchen area. From behind the door came the sound of wood being hit upon wood. Bullock was about to look through the doorway when Falconer returned with his new guest, a lean and elderly Jew.

'Peter, I would like you to meet a respected doctor and scientist, Zerach de Alemmania. We have a mutual friend in Friar Bacon.'

Bullock nodded his head at the Jew, and wondered if scientist meant magician, especially if the man knew Bacon as well as Falconer did. Zerach clutched a paper tube twisted at both ends as though it held some contents he did not wish to spill. Zerach glanced nervously at the constable, knowing who he was, and whispered anxiously to Falconer.

'I have brought what you asked of me. I only hope we can trust the friar's recipe.'

He held the tube out to Falconer, who took it gingerly, and stowed it carefully behind the barrel at one end of the room.

'I am sure that Roger was precise in his specifications. Now, you know when to act?'

The Jew nodded and shuffled to stand in one corner of the hall, as though seeking to be invisible. The next arrivals only confirmed him in his wish not to be conspicuous. A thunderous knocking at the door announced the advent of the two priests, the Prior of St Frideswide's and Edward

Petysance, priest of St Aldate's. Ushered into the room by Falconer, they looked with distaste on the cadaverous Jew who hovered in the corner of the room and demanded simultaneously of the regent master why he had summoned them to Aristotle's.

'Please. All will become clear, if you will just allow me a moment. There is someone else I would like you to talk to. Then I have a little Christmas entertainment planned. Not as elaborate as your mystery plays, Prior, but presented by the same troupe. I expect my final guests to be here very soon.'

As if prearranged, there came another knock at the door of Aristotle's Hall at that precise moment.

'If you will excuse me.'

Falconer went to welcome the new arrivals, leaving Bullock, Zerach, and the two priests standing in stony, awkward silence. The constable offered up a mute prayer that whatever Falconer had planned would be over soon.

It was very nearly finished there and then. When Falconer entered the hall followed by the ancient Jew, Bullock knew to be Rabbi Jehozadok, and some angry-looking youth he did not know, Petysance and the Prior both poured forth expressions of outrage and almost fell over each other in their attempt to escape this den of Jews. One had been bad enough; now Falconer was seeking to surround them with Christ's persecutors. Falconer simply stood squarely in the doorway and prevented their exit, his piercing blue eyes causing the priests to subside like unruly students.

'I have asked Jehozadok here to say something about the unfortunate incident in the street the other day.'

Petysance could not restrain himself and pointed an accusatory finger at Deulegard. 'That is the very youth who defiled my holy relic, and you expect me to listen to him? What possible excuse can he have for his actions?'

Deulegard in his turn waved a finger at the priest, but the rabbi placed a surprisingly strong hand on his arm and spoke first. 'Much harm has been done here by those whom I had thought to have taught better.'

Deulegard's face turned bright red, but no words would form, so incoherent with rage was he. Leaving him to splutter infuriatedly, Jehozadok blithely continued his prepared speech. 'But we all know the recklessness of youth, and I beg of you to find it in your Christian hearts to forgive their ill-considered act. It is my fault that their guidance has been so poorly handled. Alas, my advanced age has meant I have not been as strict as I should have been. I know you will forgive them, and in recompense for any damage done I am sure my community will be willing to make handsome reparation.'

Petysance's eyes lit up at the thought of payment from the Jews. Perhaps now he could build a tower as great as or even greater than the one the Prior had funded for his own church. However, it would not do to be seen to give in to the old Jew so easily, and he couched his reply in the frostiest of terms.

'Such desecration as occurred cannot easily be forgotten. And if any price is to be exacted it will only be to the greater glory of Our Lord.'

Jehozadok knew that any price Petysance exacted would be huge, and out of all proportion to the deed, but was resigned to having to pay it. He humbly nodded his head and turned his milky-eyed gaze on Falconer. He had done what the regent master had asked of him, and now he wondered what he had planned that required the presence of Deulegard. After all, the youth could have ruined any negotiations with the Christian priests — indeed had nearly done so. So Falconer must want him here for another as yet unspecified purpose. And why on earth was Zerach here too?

'I thank you all for your restraint. Now allow me to present that little diversion I promised you.'

Falconer waved his arms, and before anyone could protest and escape Agnes Cheke stepped from behind the backcloth at one end of the hall to start the play. Bullock groaned at the apparent crassness of his friend in imagining that he could hope to entertain such an ill-matched group of people, some of whom would wish not to be in the same town as the others, let alone the same room. This was going to be the most joyless celebration he had ever attended.

CHAPTER EIGHTEEN

GOD: In my blessing here I begin
The first thing in my glory and right:
Lightness and darkness? I bid both be seen,
The night in its dark, the day in its light.

The Fall of Lucifer

'My name is Old Belzibuz, with a story you to tell, Of bolden knights, and maidens fair, and one who's bound for Hell.
But ere I start this tale of old, intended you to please, I ask you all to please sit down and therefore take your ease.'

The Devil's invitation to settle down to watch the mummers' play was grudgingly obeyed by those in the room. Falconer sat in the central seat of a row the students had placed across the hall facing the backcloth of trees. The priests waited until Jehozadok, Deulegard and Zerach had chosen their seats to Falconer's right, and then sat on the two chairs furthest to his left. Bullock sat in the only remaining space, between Falconer and the Prior. Two students brought forth candles to light up the end of the hall where Agnes stood, and suddenly the painted trees took on a magical appearance, the flickering of the candlelight making it seem as though they danced in a wind that had sprung up out of nowhere. Into the light stepped Simon dressed as a Crusader knight, a large red cross prominent on his tunic.

'In comes I as bold St George, my glory is to fight.
I battle sun and moon alike — turn daytime into night.'

Bullock could feel the Prior fidgeting in his seat, clearly annoyed at wasting his time on such yokel entertainment. The constable put a firm hand on the prelate's arm and smiled grimly into the man's startled face. If Falconer wanted the Prior present for whatever reason, then the Prior would stay put. Bullock turned his gaze calmly back to the troubadours, oblivious of another person who had slipped into the room in the darkness. This was beginning to be fun.

The old familiar story unfolded, St George becoming enamoured of the King of Egypt's daughter, who in the form of Margaret Peper performed a lithe and acrobatic tumbling dance. This raised Bullock's spirits even more and brought some discreet cheers from the students who were observing from the back of the hall. Falconer turned a disapproving gaze on them and they immediately quietened down, though Bullock could discern a sparkle in the master's eyes as he looked back at the pretty saltatore. Still, the students could not restrain their disapproval when the Saracen knight, dark of feature, appeared from behind the backcloth and claimed Margaret for himself. He and St George then fought a duel while Margaret looked on. At one point in the ebb and flow of the battle, the Saracen knight retreated towards the darkness to the left side of the backcloth, and St George thrust at him with his wooden sword. A body fell to the ground, and St George claimed his prize. But then there came the cry from the right of the backcloth.

'Not so, bold George, you have not killed me yet.
You must fight on, I say, Sir Knight, your damsel for to get.'

The Saracen knight reappeared opposite the spot where his body already apparently lay and continued the fight. Bullock was mystified but delighted by this excursion from the normal play he remembered from his childhood. More of Falconer's incomprehensible doing, no doubt. After some more extravagant swordplay, the fight did reach its traditional conclusion, and the Saracen knight fell dead to a well-aimed thrust under his arm by St George. The Devil stepped forward to ask if there was a doctor present, who might cure the knight of his ills. Falconer immediately rose from his seat and stepped forward. Something told Bullock that all that had gone before had been leading up to this moment — it had Falconer's love of the histrionic all over it.

Falconer stepped over the prostrate Robert Kemp, and began to speak.

'Medicus sum et qui quae quod,
In corpore hominis — he is dead.'

The nonsense Latin brought a smile to Falconer's lips, but then he diverged from the scripted words into those of his own devising.

'Unusually I am a doctor who sees,
Not a Saracen knight but de Askeles.
Was his killer John Peper, now fled?
No indeed — de Askeles was already dead.
It matters not where John is hid,
We ask, then, who the murder did.'

Bullock could not suppress a laugh at Falconer's tortured rhymes. A solver of riddles he might be, but a maker of them? Never! Fortunately, Falconer continued without attempting any more verse.

'Prior, when I invited you here I said I would solve the deaths of Brother Adam and de Askeles. I can tell you that the person concerned in at least the latter is in this room now.'

Outraged protests from all sides were followed by uneasy glances round the room as priest stared at Jew, and the troubadours cast wary looks at each other. Kemp sat up, but stayed where he was at Falconer's feet. A stifled groan came from the back of the room.

'Up to your old tricks, I see.' The rumbling voice caused everyone to turn in that direction. It was Falconer who introduced the latecomer.

'And I welcome Master Thomas de Cantilupe to our little gathering. Somewhat late, but welcome nevertheless.'

The ex-Chancellor bowed his head in weary acknowledgement, as though giving Falconer permission to continue.

'Now why do I say that John Peper could not have killed de Askeles, when we all saw him run a sword through his body? Why — because de Askeles was already dead when John ran him through. There was barely any blood on the wounds caused by the sword, and such a cut to a living man would have bled profusely. But there was blood all over the back of the robe de Askeles wore under his costume, and a knife wound to correspond with it. So John Peper was guilty of no crime other than damaging a corpse.'

Behind Falconer Margaret gave a sob, which seemed to draw the regent master's attention. He strode over to where she stood in the midst of the exotically clad actors.

'Then we must ask who did kill de Askeles, and sit him on the throne to confuse us? Who had a reason to kill him?'

His piercing blue eyes went from sweating face to sweating face, espying the depth of guilt behind each facade.

'All of you had good reason to wish de Askeles dead. Simon and Robert, you both blamed de Askeles for the death of your fellow actor in Winchester. Agnes, you admitted you could and would kill him because of how he treated you.

And you find it difficult to account for your whereabouts at the crucial moment. Though I admit that both Simon and Robert were on stage at the moment of Brother Adam's unfortunate death. Hmm.'

He paused as though storing the facts gleaned so far, and let his gaze linger on the fearful visage of the lithesome saltatore.

'But most of all you, Margaret. You wanted to be free of his lascivious advances.'

Margaret paled, but before she could protest, Falconer pressed on.

'You hated the hold he had on you, and the fact that the only way you thought you could serve the man you loved, and were married to, was to make him the cuckold. An impossible dilemma, with only one solution. Murder.'

The young woman buried her face in her hands and sobbed. Falconer touched her gently on the shoulder, and spoke softly to her. 'Where's the carpenter's tool?'

She gazed up with tear-filled eyes. 'What tool?'

'The one the robber dropped in the wagon when you were attacked. The one Simon gave you when you asked him for a weapon to protect yourself against de Askeles.'

She looked round accusingly at Simon, who simply appeared puzzled. It was Robert who dropped his gaze guiltily, recalling what he had told the persistent regent master. Turning back to Falconer, she stammered out an excuse. 'I do not know. I must have dropped it somewhere when I was exercising.'

'Or plunged it into Brother Adam's back mistaking him for de Askeles. Perhaps it was you who then carried out the deed successfully.'

Margaret's mouth formed a perfect O of horror as Falconer once again made mental note of possible guilt. He then looked sternly at the whey-faced Fool.

'But Will, you hated the man with a simple hatred for his mistreatment of the monkey. You were on the right side of the stage at the death of both Brother Adam and Stefano de Askeles. And you have an uncontrollable temper — Agnes said so. Did you kill Stefano?'

Will's face screwed up and turned a blotchy red, like some infant with colic. The denial that came from his lips pierced the heart of all present. 'Noooo.'

Falconer patted him on the shoulder. 'I believe you, Will. For there is someone here who has had a long time to nurture his dislike of Stefano.' He stepped up to the skinny doctor, Zerach de Alemmania. 'Someone who recognized de Askeles as Stephen Askey, a student who a number of years ago was treated by a doctor in this city. When Askey refused to pay his fee, and even threatened to blacken the doctor's name with the slur of necromancy, the doctor threatened his life. Do you recall that, Master Zerach?'

Zerach stammered in amazement, while the Prior muttered something about not being surprised a Jew was at the bottom of this.

'I cannot say you saw him for sure, but there was opportunity aplenty for you to do so — the whole of Oxford knew of the troubadours' arrival soon after they came through the gates. I do know de Askeles saw you.'

The doctor's brow furrowed. 'How?'

Falconer looked across the room at an embarrassed de Cantilupe. 'You have Master Thomas here to thank for your recent arrest by the King's officers.'

De Cantilupe was quick to voice his excuses. 'It was the Prior who gave me your name.'

The Prior in his turn explained away his culpability. 'And I was given your name as a necromancer who deserved arrest and punishment.'

'And who gave you Zerach's name?'

Falconer was persistent and inexorable in his search for the truth. The Prior mumbled a name that could not be heard. When pressed again by Falconer, he blurted it out. 'De Askeles.'

Zerach's face fell. 'Yes — we did meet. I was in Fish Street when the troubadours arrived. Askey — de Askeles

— was standing behind the driver. He was fuller of face than last I had seen him, but still as drunk. I didn't think he had seen me, but I suppose he must have. I did not kill him, though.'

'Then if it was not one Jew, it was the other.'

This came from the mouth of Edward Petysance. Falconer returned his stare impassively. 'I take it you do not mean Jehozadok.'

He looked down at the ancient, who could barely stir his old bones from the chair in which he sat, let alone stab someone.

'And as for Deulegard, why should he kill de Askeles?'

The youth in question shot a surly look at Falconer as though defying him to find a reason. Petysance supplied it before the regent master could continue.

'The whole town can provide you with a reason. Everyone heard it from his own mouth after he had defiled my holy relic. A life for a life was his threat. He obviously carried it out.'

Deulegard's face turned crimson as he rose and screamed back at the little priest. 'And if I had, I would not regret it now. Solomon was a fool but he was one of my kind, and an eye for an eye is something you Christians should understand.'

Petysance's face was suffused with self-justification and he gestured at the youth as much as to say that he had confessed. Falconer stepped between them with his back to Deulegard. He spoke directly to Petysance.

'There is something in what you say. The death of Solomon is indeed the key to our search.'

Bullock was puzzled.

'Why? What has his death to do with the murder of de Askeles?'

'Perhaps nothing. But it is my experience that deaths following close on the heels of one another are intertwined in some way. We need to ask ourselves why Solomon, a solitary, harmless old graveyard-keeper, was killed at all.'

Jehozadok's piping voice interrupted. 'Remember, dear friend, I told you he claimed to have seen someone in the town meeting with a rough-looking type he thought was one of the robbers that plague us. Perhaps they saw him and wanted to close his mouth.'

'Perhaps.' Falconer did not look convinced. 'We should not dismiss it as a theory — the traitor in our midst would certainly wish to avoid being exposed. But why didn't he act sooner? No, I think Solomon's death relates to something he saw much more recently in the graveyard.'

Zerach's face turned a deathly white, and he resembled more closely than ever the skeleton his cadaverous form suggested to the Christian youths who mocked him in the street.

'Why should I kill him, when all he may have seen was me digging for saltpetre? I swear I didn't even know he had seen me.'

Falconer smiled secretively, and revealed his most startling deduction. 'Perhaps he died because he knew that de Askeles had defiled the cemetery.'

There were gasps of astonishment on all sides at this statement, and even Jehozadok raised his dimly seeing eyes to Falconer. Deulegard rose again out of his seat and thrust his face at the regent master's.

'What do you mean, defiled our cemetery?'

'When Jehozadok spoke to me about the death of old Solomon, I was puzzled about the conversation he had had earlier with the old man. As the night guardian of the Jews' cemetery, it seemed that his statement about seeing God at a graveside was a fanciful idea — perhaps the old man had been dreaming. But, Jehozadok, you assured me Solomon took his duties seriously. That he did not sleep on duty, and that he was a very literal-minded person not given to flights of fancy.'

'He was simple,' snorted Deulegard.

'Simple, maybe. But he was very clear about what he saw,' responded Jehozadok. 'I am interested in what you think he meant, William.'

'He meant exactly what he said. He said he saw God taking away one of the bodies. When you put that fact together with the fact that he had just come from watching a rehearsal of the mystery plays where de Askeles had been playing God on the stage, it is no leap of imagination to realize he meant he saw de Askeles in the cemetery.'

A small, clear voice cut through the others' expressions of derision and disbelief. Margaret stepped into the light cast by the candles.

'You could be right. I think I now understand what Stefano and John were arguing about the other day when I overheard them. When you were investigating the first attempt on Stefano's life, John wanted to tell you where he and Stefano had been at the time. But Stefano wouldn't let him. Where else could they have been that was nearly as dangerous to reveal as being suspected of murder? It must have been Stefano and John in the cemetery. John said someone had seen them — that must have been this . . . Solomon.'

'And that is why I have no doubt that it was de Askeles who killed Solomon — to keep him quiet. Pity he was unaware that he had already spoken to the rabbi.'

At Falconer's words, Jehozadok sighed. 'At least there is some justice for poor Solomon. His murderer did not escape. But what was de Askeles doing in the graveyard?'

Falconer knew his next assertion would create an uproar but pressed on. 'I realized that when Agnes told me he dabbled in selling fake holy relics. You see, he needed some bones to sell to Edward Petysance.'

He could not have caused a greater reaction in both camps in the room. Jehozadok's head dropped into his hands, but Deulegard's face became a mask of impassivity like something from the actors' property store. The Prior, at first shocked, could not prevent a smirk from crossing his lips at the horror perpetrated on his rival. The holy limb of St Eldad was nothing more than the arm-bone of some long dead Jew — what a wonderful fraud. Edward Petysance just stood stock still, his face bloodless.

It was Bullock's turn to throw his thoughts into this whirling morass of accusation and denial. 'Then if the theft from the cemetery and the sale of the bones was the reason for de Askeles's murder, it must have been you, priest, who killed him.'

'And if I say, as is true, that I had no idea of the vile act that has been perpetrated on me by these evil-minded people until now?' He stared at Agnes, Simon and Robert as though they were all accomplices to de Askeles's deed. 'Then it is clear I had no reason to kill him.'

Deulegard snorted in derision. 'And we are to take your word for it, are we?'

Bullock found himself supporting Petysance's reasoning. 'It matters little whether we believe the priest or not. He was at the front of the crowd watching the plays when de Askeles was killed, wasn't he?'

It was de Cantilupe's turn to assist. He was finding this exercise in deductive logic most stimulating, and began to understand what enticed Falconer to it.

'Let me think. We saw de Askeles playing the part of God at the end of Christ's Ascension. Then came the Last Judgement, by which time he was dead and had been placed on the throne.'

'But there was a long gap between those scenes,' added Simon Godrich. 'There always is, while we prepare the final stage.'

'And for the whole of that time,' stated Petysance triumphantly, 'I was in view of everyone present in the audience. Didn't the whole crowd see me exhorting the King to visit the holy relics of St Eldad? How could I have killed him, when I was elsewhere? And while we are casting accusations about, I would like to know who pretended to be the Virgin in my church when de Askeles concocted his "miracles" over the fake relics?' He stared at Margaret, who flushed and looked at the ground. 'If they can be involved in such a sacrilegious act, it would not surprise me if these so-called troubadours were capable of murdering their own leader. There is no honour amongst thieves, after all.'

As one, the little band of actors, except for the frightened Will Plome, surged forward angrily towards their accuser.

But Falconer stepped in their way, his arms spread wide. 'The priest has a point. He must be innocent, as he could not have been in two places at once.'

Petysance did not leave it there however, pursuing the object of his hatred. 'Then the attack on me, and de Askeles's murder, is clearly laid at this Jew's door.'

Falconer looked down at the soft leather boots on Deulegard's feet — were they the ones he had espied on the mysterious figure backstage the previous night? Could the dark robe have been the Jew's habitual garb? He had threatened to take a life, and could have known of de Askeles's nocturnal activities, though he protested ignorance and scorned Solomon's story of the appearance of God. The roomful of people, students, priests and Jews sensed his uncertainty, and it was as if no one dared breathe for fear of disturbing his concentration. What he said unleashed a series of unexpected happenings.

'Ah, if only we could ask de Askeles himself.'

Hardly were Falconer's words uttered than there came a strange hissing sound, and Bullock thought he saw a flaming torch thrown across the room. But before he could make sense of what he had seen, there was a fearful flash and a thunderclap that echoed off the walls. All those present were deafened and shocked as their senses reeled. Their nostrils were assaulted by a hellish smell of burning and some undefinable, unnatural stench. Then through the sulphurous, reeking smoke there loomed a shape. It was Stefano de Askeles dressed as God, his gilded mask staring blank-eyed and accusing at those assembled. The Prior fell to his knees uttering a prayer, but most just stood open-mouthed in horror.

The figure, as if conjured from hell, drifted across the room towards the knot of actors, and began to raise one arm. They gasped as one as the terrifying shape strode past them. A long and accusatory finger was raised in the direction of Deulegard, whose mouth dropped open despite himself. It seemed to linger for an age before the Jew, then finally the apparition pointed directly at Edward Petysance. The white-faced priest spun round and made for the door at the back of the hall. Before he could reach it, Falconer knocked aside the petrified audience like ninepins, grabbing the fleeing man's robe in his fist. Spinning Petysance around, he spat the accusation in his face.

'You did kill de Askeles, didn't you?'

The priest's face was a picture of terror, and his hands clutched the cross that hung round his neck. No words came to his trembling lips till, looking over Falconer's shoulder, he espied de Askeles's ghost seeking him out.

'Yes, yes I did,' he wailed. 'Don't let him near me, please. Please!'

The figure of God was striding towards Falconer and the priest, who raised his arms to ward off the retribution. Hovering over the cowering man, the figure raised its hands on either side of its golden head and pulled off its mask, revealing the very human face of a grinning Thomas Symon. The priest sobbed.

'You cheated me.' Then, thinking of the cause of his original downfall, he muttered, 'He cheated me, don't you see? He cheated me.'

CHAPTER NINETEEN

GOD: As I have made all things of nought,
After my will and my wishing,
My first day now have I wrought,
I give it here fully my blessing.

The Fall of Lucifer

It was the following day before Peter Bullock got to draw his flagon of ale from Falconer's barrel. The previous night had been occupied with the incarceration of Edward Petysance, and the restoration of the bones from St Aldate's Church to Jehozadok. He had not had a chance to return to Aristotle's Hall. Today was different and he was not to be diverted from his pleasures — he did not even mind when the regent master told him the barrel was from Kepeharm's inn. Despite what he knew of its source, the ale did taste sweet. He wiped the back of his hand across his mouth and leaned back on the bench. He was seated with Falconer and the small band of troubadours around the long, scarred table that had been reinstated in its central place in the hall. Pleasant smells were drifting from the kitchen, from where also came a babble of voices as Falconer's students argued over the task, unusual for them, of cooking the planned Christmas feast. The cooking odours almost, but not completely, masked the strange smell that still hung in the air from Zerach's black powder parcel. The thunderclap had been much louder than either he or Falconer had intended — clearly Friar Bacon's mixture was more powerful than they had expected.

'You already knew it was Petysance who killed de Askeles when you arranged the events of last evening, then?'

Falconer smiled secretively, not wishing to disappoint his friend. He had actually not been sure of anything last night and did not wish to admit that he had depended on histrionics to smoke out the malefactor. Bullock, meanwhile, continued to worry at the puzzle like a deer hound with a fallen stag.

'But he truly convinced me it wasn't him when he asked about the time de Askeles had been stabbed. I still don't see how he could have been both backstage killing de Askeles, then putting the body on the throne, and talking to the King as well.'

'It's simple — he wasn't. Because de Askeles was not murdered when we all originally thought he was.'

Agnes leaned forward with interest. 'When was he killed, then?'

'During the enactment of Christ's Passion.' Falconer was emphatic. 'I knew I had witnessed a murder — yet again — it's just that there was no body this time. The mysterious figure from out of the crowd was Petysance. When you and I spoke, Agnes, de Askeles was already dead.'

'But we saw Stefano after that. He spoke to us when he climbed the ladder backstage, remember?'

'No. Someone dressed as God grunted at us. We just assumed it was de Askeles because it was normally him under the mask. Remember my trick with the Saracen knight last evening? Those watching thought St George had killed him when a body fell at one side of the backcloth, only to have Robert reappear at the other side unscathed. The body was Thomas dressed in similar clothes, and the audience saw what they expected to see. We expected to see de Askeles and so we did. But it was Petysance dressed up as God we saw, and by then he had already killed de Askeles.'

Falconer shivered. 'You said de Askeles must have gone to God's throne in drunken error. And you were partly right. Petysance must have dragged the body of de Askeles backstage and sat him up on the throne, before donning God's robe and mask himself.'

Agnes thought for a little, staring into space and trying to recall that fateful night.

'I do recall thinking for a moment that it was not Stefano — there was something odd about his walk, and he did not seem as tall. But then I forgot about it in the relief at seeing him get to his place on time. But why take the risk of discovery at all?'

'So that he could fool us into thinking de Askeles was still alive. And place himself elsewhere at the supposed time of death. He is a very quick thinker, our angry priest. Resurrecting de Askeles from the dead was a risk, but one worth it to throw us off the scent. John's swordplay was an unexpected but additional benefit. And that should have been the end of the matter. The trouble was with the state of the body, was it not, Peter?'

Bullock coughed non-committally and took a deep draught from his ale. He had not really understood what Falconer's and Bonham's examination of the body had revealed to them, besides there being an additional wound. But he was not going to reveal his ignorance. Fortunately Falconer proceeded eagerly with his story.

'If he had been killed shortly before we lifted him off the throne, either by John Peper or by someone else in the time between the Ascension and the Last Judgement, his blood would not have had time to pool in his lower extremities before we laid him flat. It would have pooled across his whole back. The fact that the blood showed he had been in a seated position for some time after death meant the body had been sitting up for some time.

'After Petysance had played the part of God, it was simple for him to slip back down the ladder and dress de Askeles in the white robe and mask. There was no reason for anyone else to be behind the scenery at the time. Unfortunately, he couldn't get the robe fully down the corpse's back, which had already stiffened in the chair. That explains why the blood from de Askeles's death wound was on the hem, and the cloth was caked in bloody folds. Oh, and he made one other error — de Askeles's eyes were closed.'

'What does that show?' asked Agnes with curiosity.

'As he was violently murdered his eyes would have been wide open. The murderer must have closed them. And it is the instinct of a priest when faced with a body to close the eyes before the death rigor sets in. Even that little matter pointed to Petysance as the killer.'

'Why kill at such a time, with so much chance of discovery? If he knew about de Askeles's trickery, why had he not taken action before?'

'Because he did not know before. It was only during Christ's Betrayal that John betrayed de Askeles as a way of getting back at him. Then the priest acted on the spur of the moment, using the chaos behind the stage to hide his deed. No doubt he was provoked by de Askeles when he confronted him, too.'

'Wait a moment, master.' It was Margaret who broke in now. 'How do you know John told him?'

Falconer smiled ruefully.

'Ah. Because I spoke to him.'

Margaret gasped.

'He is here?'

'Yes. You see, one of my students heard some noises early yesterday morning in my neighbour's yard. They were coming from the pigsty, and as the previous occupant is going to grace our table today it was clear it could not have been the pig. I went down to investigate and found a very frightened and cold John Peper huddled in the corner of the sty. After I managed to persuade him he was not a fugitive in my eyes, he agreed to accept my hospitality.'

At that point, a sheepish John Peper stepped into the hall, dressed in borrowed and rather ill-fitting clothes, and unsure of the reception he might get from his wife and fellows. He should not have been concerned — they rose from the table and clustered around him, Will performing a clumsy somersault in his joy. They stood back a little as he held out a tentative hand to Margaret, who unhesitatingly grasped it and drew her husband back to the table with her.

A pitcher of ale, drawn from the barrel, was passed around the happy band of revellers. But Falconer was surprised to see a frown still on the constable's face.

'Is something still troubling you, Peter?'

'If Petysance only had cause to kill de Askeles the other night, then who attempted to kill him earlier, when Brother Adam died in his stead? It could not have been John because we now know where he was.'

His sharp eyes bore into the embarrassed Peper, who had hoped that his act of grave robbery had been forgotten. Falconer leaned back and explained. 'Thinking that the two killings were carried out by the same person only confused matters. When I realized they were not, the scales fell from my eyes. It was you, Peter, after all, who said de Askeles had more enemies than Emperor Frederick.'

Bullock had no intention of reminding Falconer that he himself had said only the previous night that two murders, carried out so close in time, were likely to be associated. He did not want another lecture. He did look carefully around the room and whispered in his friend's ear that those present were still then suspects for the first murder. After all, the carpenter's tool Margaret obtained from Godrich was still missing, and she could not prove it was not the chisel that killed the monk.

Falconer laughed and fished an object out of his purse. 'I suppose you mean this.' He opened his hand and in it lay a long pointed sort of bodkin with a well-worn wooden handle. Bullock looked at the bradawl in astonishment.

'Where did you find it?'

'In the bottom of the monkey's cage, along with a lot of other gewgaws. Ham is obviously a hoarder of objects that take his fancy. He must have stolen it from Margaret, so the weapon she had and the deadly chisel were not one and the same. I found it this morning, by the way — like you, I wanted to clear up the matter of Brother Adam, which we seemed to have forgotten in the excitement of last night.'

'Then if it wasn't Margaret or John Peper, who was it?'

Peter prayed it was not Agnes, for whom he had a certain affection.

'I told you all along to check the carpenter. Yesterday, I spoke again to his wife, poor woman, and she admitted he had come home the day of Brother Adam's death threatening to kill someone who had shamed him in front of his fellows. I imagine that must have been de Askeles. The man was a drunkard and hot-tempered enough to carry out his threats. She even showed me a bloody jerkin he left behind when he deserted her. I have no doubt it's Brother Adam's blood. He was also earning money to spend on drink by revealing travellers' movements to the robbers in our vicinity.'

He put out a hand to stop the constable who was rising from the table.

'Don't worry. I have already passed on his name to the King's officers, so he will be taken and will pay for all his crimes. If the robbers do not despatch him first — as a fugitive himself, he's no longer any use to them.'

Suddenly the kitchen door burst open and Thomas led out the students who had toiled there, singing lustily.

'Lordings, Christmas loves good drinking,
Wines of Gascoigne, France, Anjou,
English ale that drives out thinking,
Prince of liquors old or new.
All the sweets that love bestows,

Endless pleasures wait on those
Who, like vassals brave and true,
Give to Christmas homage due.'

With that, two students emerged from the kitchen, pink-faced and sweating. Between them, on a battered pewter platter, they bore a steaming pig's head with something held between its teeth. They brought it to the head of the table, where Falconer sat, and he extracted his eye-lenses to examine the delicacy the pig had in its mouth. It was a book. Falconer roared with laughter — he knew what the text would be and hoped Aristotle did not mind.

EPILOGUE

History books do not record a reason for the attack by Jews on the clergy in 1268. Persecuted and hated as they were in England at the time, it perhaps should be no surprise that they would retaliate against persistent attacks on them by their host community. What is recorded is the compensation exacted from the Jews for their action. The offenders had to atone by setting up a great marble cross in the street, and by providing a replacement silver crucifix to be used in processions on ceremonial days. Nothing more was heard of the holy arm of St Eldad.

Much as he thought, King Henry had to resolve the matter of the disinherited knights himself. His son, Edward, used hurdles and planks to build bridges on to the isle of Ely and overcame the rebels.

Of the little band of troubadours — Will Plome, Margaret and John Peper, Agnes Cheke, Simon Godrich and Robert Kemp — there is nothing chronicled. Such is the fate of little people who are not involved in affairs of church or state, nor in the running of an important monastery or priory. They may appear as magicians to the common herd and may have a profound impact on their mundane lives, bringing a short moment of pleasure. But their deeds are not deemed worthy of permanent record.

Rabbi Jehozadok and Zerach de Alemmania both died and were buried in the Jewish cemetery outside East Gate before the general expulsion of the English Jews by King Edward in 1290. All trace of Deulegard, Cressant and the other Jews is lost at this time.

Thomas de Cantilupe never quite recovered the official status he had enjoyed as Chancellor of England for the rebel Simon de Montfort. However, his diplomatic and devious skills allowed him to become a close adviser to de Montfort's enemy King Henry, and to his son Edward I.

Richard Bonham paid the price for his clandestine curiosity and died of typhus soon after the events described here. It is thought he contracted the disease from an infected body he was anatomizing.

Thomas Symon remained at Oxford, becoming in his turn a regent master of the Faculty of Arts despite further involvements with William Falconer that threatened to divert him from his studies. He later played a part in the founding of University College.

Peter Bullock died a warrior's death as he might have wished. His soldier's instinct deserted him for once, and he stepped in the way of a rusty sword wielded by a student in the midst of a pitched battle between northern and Welsh clerks. But not before he was involved in many more mysteries unraveled by his friend Regent Master Falconer.

William Falconer was to have many further adventures, occasioned by his insatiable curiosity. He is said to have returned to travelling later in life, reaching as far as Cathay, or China. He did finally make contact again with his life-long friend and mentor, Friar Roger Bacon. Whether he completed his *Summa Philosophiae* is not known, as no properly attributable text exists.

THE END

THE JOFFE BOOKS STORY

We began in 2014 when Jasper agreed to publish his mum's much-rejected romance novel and it became a bestseller.

Since then we've grown into the largest independent publisher in the UK. We're extremely proud to publish some of the very best writers in the world, including Joy Ellis, Faith Martin, Caro Ramsay, Helen Forrester, Simon Brett and Robert Goddard. Everyone at Joffe Books loves reading and we never forget that it all begins with the magic of an author telling a story.

We are proud to publish talented first-time authors, as well as established writers whose books we love introducing to a new generation of readers.

We have been shortlisted for Independent Publisher of the Year at the British Book Awards three times, in 2020, 2021 and 2022, and for the Diversity and Inclusivity Award at the Independent Publishing Awards in 2022.

We built this company with your help, and we love to hear from you, so please email us about absolutely anything bookish at feedback@joffebooks.com

If you want to receive free books every Friday and hear about all our new releases, join our mailing list: www.joffebooks.com/contact

And when you tell your friends about us, just remember: it's pronounced Joffe as in coffee or toffee!

ALSO BY IAN MORSON

WILLIAM FALCONER MEDIEVAL MYSTERIES
Book 1: FALCONER'S CRUSADE
Book 2: FALCONER'S JUDGEMENT
Book 3: FALCONER AND THE FACE OF GOD

Printed in Great Britain
by Amazon

62136392R00129